Praise for *Riding on Duke's Train*

"In schools where students are lucky enough to experience classroom jazz studies, this title, combining rich musical history and a "you are there" approach, is a natural."
—*Kirkus*

"This enthralling book is an adventure story with a smart, historical framework, one that has been lauded by jazz critics and those who knew the Duke."
—*ForeWord Reviews*, Winter 2012 **Recommended Books for Kids**

"From reading this novel, many young readers here and around the world will be impelled to hear Duke's music and to read more and more about the international language that jazz has become. Duke used to say that the individual sound of a musician revealed his soul. Mick Carlon is a 'soul' storyteller."
—**Nat Hentoff**, jazz critic and children's book author

"Robert Louis Stevenson kept sufficiently in touch with the child in himself to speak to all ages. Mick Carlon possesses that same quality: a clarity of diction; impatience with literariness; and a youthful impatience to get on with the story. Stevenson would surely have approved of 'Riding on Duke's Train,' a ripping good yarn that plunges the reader into the world of Duke Ellington and the Europe and America of 1939."
—**Brian Morton**, author of *The Penguin Guide to Jazz*

Travels WITH Louis

Also by the author

Riding on Duke's Train

Travels WITH Louis

Mick Carlon

A LeapKids Book
Leapfrog Kids
Leapfrog Press
Fredonia, New York

A LeapKids Book
Leapfrog Kids

Published in 2012 in the United States by
Leapfrog Press LLC
PO Box 505
Fredonia, NY 14063
www.leapfrogpress.com

Printed in the United States of America

Distributed in the United States by
Consortium Book Sales and Distribution
St. Paul, Minnesota 55114
www.cbsd.com

First Edition

ISBN: 978-1-935248-35-4

Library of Congress Cataloging-in-Publication Data

TK

Manufactured by Thomson-Shore, Dexter, MI (USA); RMA583DR528, July, 2012

"To my three ladies: Lisa, Hannah, and Sarah. And with great thanks and appreciation to Jack Bradley, Nat Hentoff, and Brian Morton. Thanks, lads!"

List of References

One

Corona, Queens: Early August 1959. Dusk drenched in summer shadows. A baseball diamond in the neighborhood. Old Mrs. Fontaine calling for one of her cats. Soft front-stoop voices and the bells of a Good Humor Ice Cream truck.

Since the boys who played ball daily on this field were only twelve years old, no windows had yet been shattered.

"It's too dark," said Fred. "I can't see the ball anymore."

"Aw!" scoffed Mark. "Our Freddie just wants to run home and play his little horn."

"You don't see Willie Mays playing no horn," said Steve, sprawling in the grass behind the pitcher's mound.

Fred grinned. He knew his friends envied his musical talent—*and* his trumpet teacher.

"When's Louis getting home?" asked Mark, a husky boy with enormous eyes.

"Next week sometime," said Fred.

"Where'd he go to this time?"

"Africa."

"Oh, man—imagine *that*!" said Steve.

"Man, I'd love to go there!" said Mark.

"And see all those ladies wearing no shirts!" said Fred.

"Aaaaaaawwww!"

Their hands behind their heads, the three boys stared up at the dusky purple sky. Mothers were calling in the little ones and the sounds of radios and televisions spilled out from the nearby homes.

"My dad says that when he was a kid, Louis Armstrong was *it*," said Steve. "That Pops was the cleanest, sharpest dude *any*where. He said that you bought his records the *second* those babies came out."

Fred smiled with pride. For a moment no one spoke.

"Anyone have any money?"

"Yeah," said Steve. "I have a buck fifty left over from my birthday."

"Let's go to Fat Pete's," said Fred, leaping up. "Steve, my man, you're treating us to some ice cream."

As a jet from LaGuardia Airport headed out across the Atlantic, the three friends dashed off to Fat Pete's Ice Cream Parlor.

Two

"Is that you, son?" asked Big Fred from the living room. Only the lamp standing behind his favorite chair lit the room. A pile of newspapers lay at his feet and some jazz played softly on the radio.

"Yeah, Dad."

"There's a postcard for you on the kitchen table."

On the postcard two gazelles were sprinting across the African plain. The back was covered with Louis' curlicued handwriting. As he climbed the stairs to his bedroom, Little Fred read:

Brother Fred:

I'm playing my horn for the people and they're giving old Pops back plenty of love. Speaking of love, Miss Lucille and I are sending you and your dad plenty from across the seas! See you soon!
Red Beans & Ricely Yours,

Louis
P.S. Now save some of that good old Fat Pete's ice cream for me, you hear?

From beneath his bed Fred pulled the shoebox that held all of Louis' postcards. You name the city—Paris, London, Rome, Boise, Rio de Janeiro, Hyannis, Mexico City, Milwaukee, Montreal, Providence, Venice—Louis had played them all. To his collection Fred added the galloping gazelles.

A battered old trumpet—a horn that had belonged to his grandfather—stood waiting on the night table. Not a day passed without Fred practicing his music. A warm breeze was stirring the curtains. Standing by the window, he blew some soft, sad, sighing blues. To Fred, this was the only reason to play music: to release his feelings, to let out his emotions, whether they were Friday afternoon joyous or Monday morning lowdown.

A knock on the door.

"Come in."

His father entered. Since his wife's death three years before, Big Fred tried every day to be there for his son. Yet he also knew when to give the boy his space. Along with playing music, Little Fred's happiest times were spent playing catch in the evenings with his father.

"Sounds good, son, real good. You sure can play them blues." He sat down on the end of the bed.

"Thanks." A question occurred to the boy. "Dad, why is Louis so good to us?"

Big Fred smiled his warm, gap-toothed smile. "Because a long time ago Louis and your grandfather—my father—were dear friends. They played music together all over New Orleans and then in the summers they played on those riverboats that chug up and down the Mississippi."

Sometimes he looks so sad, thought Little Fred. *Always remember that he misses her, too. You're not the only one.* He looked over at his horn—battered, bruised, and tarnished in the lamplight. For a moment he pictured it in the hands of his grandfather—a man he had never known—in a sweltering dance hall in 1918 New Orleans. Lovely ladies swayed in front of the bandstand, their reflections captured in the horn's bell.

"How come you never played?" he asked his father. "Why did you give it to me?"

His father smiled. "Some people are born with certain talents and some people aren't. I'm in the last category as far as music goes. I tried—but I just didn't have it. You, on the other hand, have a true talent, son. It's a pleasure when I'm downstairs reading the papers and I hear you playing. It's better than the radio these days."

Remember how they would laugh together in the living room? Now all he does is read at night. Some Saturday nights he even forgets that Gunsmoke is on.

"How old were you when Grandpa died?" asked Little Fred.

"As old as you are now—twelve."

"You've never told me what he died of."

Big Fred took a deep breath. "That's because I felt you weren't old enough yet to know. But you're growing up into a thoughtful young man. Don't think I haven't noticed." Another deep breath. "You ever notice how I don't touch alcohol?" The boy nodded. "That's because I saw it kill my father. I saw how alcohol poisoned his relations with my mother, how it smothered his music."

"He died from drinking?"

"Yes—and I swore to myself as a boy that I wouldn't let alcohol ruin my life, too."

Father and son were quiet. In the distance a siren wailed.

"And that's when Louis stepped up to the plate. God knows he didn't have to. He and my father had been out of touch for years. But Pops took a genuine interest in my mother and me. Every month a check would arrive in the mail to pay for our rent and groceries. And then when I turned sixteen he began taking me out on the road with his band in the summers.

Paid me ridiculous amounts of money to simply set up some microphones. The rest of the time I explored foreign cities and listened to Louis' music. I couldn't *believe* the money he paid me. I'd mail most of it back to my mother. I don't know where I'd be without that man." Big Fred gently squeezed the back of the boy's neck. "You know he loves you like a grandson. You should see his eyes light up when he sees my father's old horn in your hands."

"But Louis' eyes are *always* lit up," said Little Fred.

His father laughed. "That's so! Can't deny that. Some folks are born geniuses and others are born nobility. Pops is both. Good night, son. I love you."

"Love you, too, Dad."

Little Fred played his grandfather's horn for at least an hour before he fell asleep. Downstairs his father read his newspapers and enjoyed the music.

Three

On this steamy August night the drone of crickets nearly drowned out the distant sounds of car-horns and sirens. Little Fred and his father sat reading in the living room, a recording of Louis Armstrong's Hot Fives playing softly on the phonograph. On the last day of school the boy's English teacher, Mr. Kendall, had given him a hard-cover copy of Richard Wright's autobiography, *Black Boy*, which he was now reading.

"I can't believe this!" said Little Fred.

His father looked up from his book, a biography of Thomas Jefferson. "What?"

"Richard's a teenager and he can't even take a book out of the *library*! He has to find a sympathetic white man to write a note saying that Richard is taking the book out for *him*!"

"This is happening in Memphis, right?"

"Yes."

"I'm about ten years younger than Mister Wright and you know that I lived for a spell in Knoxville, on the other side of Tennessee, and it was exactly the same. The trouble was I couldn't find a sympathetic white man to write me a note."

"That's crazy."

Father and son read silently for several minutes. Then: "Dad, why do we read so much? Steve and Mark can't stand it."

"Do you enjoy it?"

"Playing my trumpet comes first, then playing catch with you, then playing baseball with Steve and Mark. But after all that, I guess reading is my favorite thing to do."

Big Fred smiled. "I picked up my love of reading from my mama, God rest her soul. I've told you a thousand times how my father was always on the road, so that left Mama and me on our own most of the time. Morning, noon, and night that good woman read to me—and if someone does that to a child, chances are that he grows up loving books and all they can unlock."

"Did you read to me when I was little?"

"Don't you remember? Mostly it was your mother, but I'd try to sneak in a book or three. But as an English professor, your mother was in charge of that department. At least until she became sick."

As Little Fred read more of *Black Boy*, he squirmed in his seat. "Aw, man!"

"What now?"

"The ten-thousandth white person in this book just called Richard a *nigger*."

Big Fred put down his book. "Has anyone ever called you that, son?"

"No. I've heard it being used—but it was never at me."

"Well, it pains me to say this, but prepare yourself. Sooner or later, you'll have that word thrown at you. Just don't put yourself in danger because of it."

For a moment the boy was afraid to ask the question: "Have *you* ever been called it?"

"Growing up in Tennessee, you heard that word as often as you swallowed your own saliva. Times are changing for the better, but it's only a matter of time until—"

A sudden trumpet blast rattled the walls.

"I *know* you two rascals are at home!" called a growly, gruff, bullfroggy voice from the front stoop. "Open up or I'll huff and I'll puff and I'll blow this door down! *Heh heh heh!*"

Louis was home.

Four

Lifting the latch on the front door, Little Fred fairly flew into the arms of his old friend.

"*Heh, heh, heh,*" laughed Louis. "I missed you, too, Pops!"

"Hello, gentlemen," said Mrs. Armstrong, a lovely lady who smelled of rosewater. "I was for ringing the doorbell, but Louis said his trumpet would have more of an effect."

Louis chuckled like a bullfrog at midnight. "We horn players always answer to the call—don't we, Little Fred?"

Big Fred embraced the old musician. "You haven't been starving yourself over in Africa, have you, Pops?"

Patting his stomach, Louis smiled the smile of a mischievous angel—a smile known the world over. He was dressed in Bermuda shorts, white socks, tan sandals, and a Dizzy Gillespie t-shirt. Perspiration glistened off his balding head. *Look at him*, thought Little Fred. *He's short, kind of fat, and he's losing his hair. But he fills up the room like a giant in a fairy tale. How?*

After Big Fred brewed some coffee, the friends sat in the living room and talked.

"Ah! *Struttin' With Some Barbecue*," said Louis, nodding at the phonograph. "What year was that? 1928?"

"December, 1927," said Little Fred.

"You're one hip little cat, Fred. I missed you, brother. *Heh, heh, heh*. Man, Africa is one swinging place. One evening in Accra—that's the capital of Ghana— over ten thousand good folks were there to greet Pops and his Lucille. The moon was full and those fine African people carried me and my lady from the airport to the stadium on two bamboo chairs! I'm being carried along, playing my horn, and everyone is chanting, *Louis! Louis! Louis!* Miss Lucille is being carried along behind me, taking care not to display her delicate bloomers, *heh, heh!*"

"You had nothing to worry about in your baggy old pants," said Mrs. Armstrong. "We ladies have it more difficult when we're being carried through African cities—on bamboo chairs, no less!"

"Hmm, fine coffee, Big Fred," said Louis. "Man, you two should've *heard* that night's show! They told us that over *one hundred thousand* people were packed into that stadium! Good Lord! I was certainly wishing my two Freds were there. The African moon was big and buttery and we just played that good old good music all night for the cats. You should've *seen* them all dancing—one of the most beautiful sights I've ever laid eyes on, man!"

"But you're forgetting the most astonishing part," said Mrs. Armstrong. "At a party after the show, Louis saw a woman who was the mirror image of his mother."

"That's so. She looked so like my Mayann that I got all choked up. It's strange but I do seem to resemble folks from that part of Africa: real dark skin, wide nose, built close to the ground but, *heh, heh, powerful.* Yeah!"

"Oh, hush yourself," said Mrs. Armstrong.

"*Dang!*" declared Louis. "I do believe I left the car door open. Back in a flash, folks."

As Big Fred poured more coffee for Mrs. Armstrong, she said, "He missed you both very much. 'I do wish the boys were here,' he kept saying."

Suddenly Louis had returned, smiling slyly, his arms behind his back.

"I hated to lie, Little Fred, but I knew that car door was closed all the time. Old Pops isn't *that* old yet. I just wanted to grab this fellow."

23

Louis held out his hands. In them gleamed a shining silver trumpet. The boy did not know what to say. *Say, 'Thank you,' dummy*, he thought. "Thank you, Louis," he said.

"We bought this old devil in Paris. I was strolling down the Boulevard de Clichy like a true Frenchman with my lovely lady on my arm when I spotted him in a shop window. Lucille gave old Pops a nudge and we made the shop owner's day, *heh, heh*. It's all yours, Fred."

For a moment the boy felt guilty. "Dad, do you mind if I use this one as well as Grandpa's?" he asked.

"Are you kidding?" said Big Fred. "That battered old thing is ready for a museum."

Raising the gleaming trumpet to his lips, Fred played a chorus of Clifford Brown's *Joy Spring*. The notes seemed to spring with new life from the horn. Louis sat back, a satisfied grin on his face.

"Man, that's *tasty*, Pops—mighty fine. Now I *know* my francs weren't wasted. My ears are also telling me loud and clear that you've been practicing."

"Every day."

"Just like your granddaddy," said Louis. "Old Henry *lived* for that horn. Little Fred, it's a shame you never met your granddaddy because that cat was a *rascal*! Am I speaking the truth, Big Fred?"

The boy's father nodded.

Louis sat back, closing his eyes. "I'll never forget the evening I met him. I was about ten years old, scrounging up bottles and rags and scraps of iron for the Karnofsky family."

Little Fred loved when his old friend became lost in a story. "Who were they, Louis?" he asked, settling back with his new trumpet in his arms, ready for a tale.

Five

"I never told you about the Karnofskys? You sure? *Hmm* . . . could've sworn I did. Anyways, they were a beautiful family who took me under their wing when I was a little bitty thing.

"My daddy split the day I was born and my mama Mayann was usually out working for a buck, so I guess the Karnofskys could see that I was a little lost soul. They were the first Jewish folks I ever met. Take a look at this." Reaching beneath his shirt, Louis pulled out a necklace with a Star of David medallion. "I always wear this to show how much I love the good Jewish people.

"Now the Karnofsky sons, Alex and Morris, were junk peddlers and I spent my days helping them gather and sell their wares. They paid me a living wage (which I naturally brought home to Mayann) and Mrs. Karnofsky always had hot heaping meals of matzos waiting for us when we were finished for the day.

"Alex and Morris thought that maybe little Louis (because I *was* a cute little cat, *heh heh!)* could attract some attention to the junk wagon they pushed through the neighborhood. Now I wasn't hip to yelling so one day I plopped down an entire *dime*—imagine that!—for a simple tin horn. I'd march in front of the Karnofsky wagon blowing for all I was worth! I grew quite good on it, too, if I do say so myself—and I do! The very first song I ever learned to play was 'Home, Sweet Home'—but soon I could play all the popular tunes along with some New Orleans hymns. All the stuff the people loved. So they'd hear Little Louis blowing his horn and the women would rush out of their cribs to buy a few pins or maybe sell a bottle.

"The Karnofskys knew that you have to encourage the little ones or they give up. They applauded me every time I blew that cheap horn, told me that I had a gift. They could see (and hear) that I had music in my soul.

"By and by I began to wonder what I would sound like on a *real* horn. One rainy morning we saw an old beat up B-flat cornet in a pawnshop window. *Ha!* I even recall the spot: at the corner of Rampart and Perdido streets. But, man, it cost a whole *five dollars!* So guess what those two brothers did? Those generous cats advanced me two dollars on my salary, then I saved fifty cents a week until I could buy that baby. Boy, was I a happy kid! I *slept* with that horn, you bet your bottom!"

I know what he means, thought Little Fred. *I'm sleeping with my new horn tonight.*

Louis' eyes were moist. "I don't know where I would've landed without that beautiful family." He blew his nose. "Sorry, folks. Just those old memories catching up with an old cat. Now, where was I?"

"The night you met my father," said Big Fred.

"That's right! So I'm heading down Canal Street to the river to see if I can nab some pickings for the Karnofskys when suddenly I hear some cat just *wailing* on his horn. The moon is huge and rippling across the Mississippi and the music is just *killing* me it's so strong and soulful. So I creep up and see this little bitty cat, like me. I introduce myself and Henry and I were soul friends from that moment on."

Little Fred tried to picture the grandfather he had never known. "Do I have his personality?" he asked.

Louis looked the boy up and down. "No, sir, I would say *no*. You're more like your daddy—clear thinking and right minded. Henry was always on fire, always planning on—"

"How to grab his next bottle," said Big Fred.

Louis winced. "Why, yes, son, I suppose that's so. Old Henry hurt the people closest to him, didn't he?

I don't have to tell *you* that."

Little Fred was surprised to hear Louis address his father as *son*.

"I'm sorry," said Big Fred. "I didn't mean to spoil the party. It's just that he could've been a much better father to me—and a better husband to my mother."

Louis reached over to squeeze Big Fred's arm. "No reason to apologize, son. You're *right*. He *should*'ve been the kind of father you are to your son. But Henry was simply not the man you are, Big Fred. That's a fact. But he wasn't an evil man, either—just weak. I say a prayer for him every day."

For only the second time in his life, Little Fred saw tears in his father's eyes. "I do, too," said Big Fred before excusing himself from the room.

"Your dad is one of the finest men I know," said Louis. "He hasn't had it easy. Neither of you have."

"I know," said Little Fred. "I try to help out around here. Every day I vacuum one room. It only takes about ten minutes. That way the house is staying clean and when Dad gets home he can relax with his papers."

Mrs. Armstrong smiled. "You're a good boy, Fred, and a true comfort to your father. I'm sure your mother is proud of both of you."

Is she? Is she watching me right now?

Standing up, Louis slapped his palms together.

29

"So! How about a lesson tomorrow morning?"

To divert attention from the tears filling his eyes, Little Fred blew a flurry of notes on his new trumpet. "What time?"

"Say nine sharp—right after a pancake breakfast cooked up smokin' hot by Miss Lucille."

Soon Big Fred returned, sitting in his favorite chair. "I'm sorry. I overreacted."

"No need to apologize for honest emotions, son," said Louis. "We're all family here."

Big Fred looked his son in the eyes. "My father let me down a thousand times and a thousand ways, Fred, and I've sworn to myself that I'll never do the same to you."

"You never have, Dad." *Don't cry, you idiot! Push those tears down!* "You guys, I'm kind of tired. I'm going to hit the hay. Thank you so much, Louis and Mrs. Armstrong, for my trumpet. It's perfect. Goodnight."

"Goodnight, son."

"See you at nine sharp, Pops!"

In his room Fred placed his grandfather's horn on the night table. His new trumpet from Paris, however, was laid gently beside his pillow. *Man, it's beautiful. Just think. This baby was actually in Paris . . . Mom always wanted to go to Paris.* A warm breeze fluttered the curtains. From outside floated the distant sound of a police car's siren. *Someone's in trouble.* Climbing into bed and closing his eyes, he could hear the voices of the adults downstairs. *Remember when you could hear Mom and Dad talking downstairs? Remember how much they laughed?*

"How are things at work?" he could hear Louis ask.

"Oh, fine. Since we all need electricity there's never a restful moment at the plant. But they gave me a raise last month. We're doing well."

"If you ever need some bread," said Louis.

"No, Pops—but thanks. We're doing okay."

"That dear boy's college money is already nestled away, you know that."

"Sometimes . . . I just can't believe your generosity."

Little Fred could hear the old musician's bullfrog chuckle: "If I didn't squirrel that bread away, Miss Lucille would spend it all on fancy clothes and open-toed shoes, *heh, heh!*"

Right before he drifted off, he heard Mrs. Armstrong's voice: "Are you dating at all?"

"No. Lorraine was the only woman for me. You know that, Lucille. My life is now wrapped up only in that boy."

In his dreams Little Fred met his mother and once again spoke with her. Sadly, in the morning he could not recall what she had said.

Six

The Armstrongs' brick house at 34-56 107th Street was three blocks from Little Fred's. As he strolled over, his new trumpet beneath his arm, the early morning cool spoke of back-to-school sales and the smell of burning leaves. *Don't worry*, he thought. *Still four weeks of summer left.*

"Good day, Pops!" said Louis, still in aqua pajamas, seated at the kitchen table reading the morning paper.

"Sit down, Fred," said Mrs. Armstrong. "Your pancakes will be ready in a jiffy."

"Now I've already run this by your father," said Louis, "but I don't want to bore you. What are your plans today?"

"Steve, Mark and I are playing homerun derby at the field," said Fred. "You know, the usual."

Louis swallowed a forkful of pancakes. "The All Stars and I are gigging tonight at the Village Vanguard.

I have to head into town this afternoon to deal with some business. Feel like heading in with me and staying for the show?"

"Are you kidding? I can play baseball any day."

"Then it's settled, Pops."

After breakfast, the two retired to Louis' second floor den. Filled with framed posters and photographs, the room was the old musician's refuge.

"I'm going to grab a shower and get dressed," said Louis. "Just make yourself at home."

An ancient typewriter sat at an oak desk, waiting to be used for yet another of Louis' single-spaced letters mailed out regularly to friends and acquaintances around the world. Hundreds of albums and home-made reel-to-reel tapes were nestled into shelves built right into the walls. Each tape lay inside a cardboard box hand-decorated (with photographs and newspaper clippings) by Louis himself. Noticing that a tape was already set up in Louis' reel-to-reel machine, Fred pressed a red button. Immediately the room was filled with the scratchy, jousting horns of a young Louis and his mentor, Joe "King" Oliver. Settling back in an easy chair, Fred closed his eyes and listened to several songs.

"Now that would be *Dipper Mouth Blues*, recorded on April 6, 1923." Louis was freshly dressed in a blue shirt, Bermuda shorts, white socks and his favorite tan sandals.

"You even remember the date?" asked the boy.

"Nope! It says so right here on the box, *heh, heh*. But I *do* remember that morning. The band and I— that would be King Oliver's Creole Jazz Band—had played 'til past three in the morning at the old Lincoln Gardens. But we were up—washed and ready—by six bells. We loaded up our instruments (and our selves, of course) into two old Model T Fords. The studio, I recall, was right by some railroad tracks in Richmond, Indiana—not too far a ride from Chicago—and my man Joe Oliver complimented my shoes. Them old Ku Klux Klan devils had been riding around the area, causing mischief, so we hightailed it right back to Chicago after the session."

The two sat back and listened to the ancient music.

"*Mmmm*, that was sweet," said Louis after the song had ended. "You know, Little Fred, there's no better way to earn your living in this world than by playing music. Just think: you're making yourself and others happy at the same time—a*nd* making some bread. Now let's have a lesson."

Louis' lessons were fun.

"First off, you have to take care of your chops—your lips and mouth, y'understand. They're your bread and butter, so baby those babies. Then—" Louis picked up his trumpet. "—you have to love your horn. This old fellow has been mighty good to old Louis. Gave me this fine home and introduced me to thousands of beautiful folks. So love and *respect* yourself and your instrument, Pops."

For months the two had been studying harmony and Fred felt he was finally unlocking the key. "It can be a beast to master," explained Louis, "but once you master harmony it's one of music's true beauties. Simply relax and try to nestle *inside* the music. It's like jumping from stone to stone across a stream. If you think *too* hard about it—like about how slippery and slimy some of those stones look—you'll freeze up and fall in. But if you simply trust, *let go*, and blow, some mighty, *mighty* things can happen. Alright, let's try *Struttin' With Some Barbecue*."

"Here goes," said Little Fred, raising his new horn to his lips. *Just let go*, he told himself. Pouring his soul into the music, he was surprised to find himself weaving skillfully through Louis' notes. For several minutes the music flowed effortlessly. *Man, it's like flying!*

Then came the musical crash. *Aw, that stank!*

"Ouch!" said Louis. "*That* was a clunker, Pops. But there isn't a musician on God's earth who hasn't played several thousand of those clams. Now climb back on that horse and *blow!*"

Man, this is fun! People who never play music don't know what they're missing. Imagine spending your entire life playing music. Louis does it . . . his whole life is music.

Why couldn't I do it, too? Yeah, I know one good reason why. . . .

The old man and the boy played music all morning long. At times Fred felt as if he had entered the "sweet spot" (as Louis put it)—the place where the music flowed naturally. *It's like hitting a solid line drive into left field.*

"That was fine, Fred—at times quite tasty. But if you *really* want to learn this music, be prepared to be learning your *entire life*—and that's the truth."

After a lunch of tuna fish sandwiches and tomato soup, they were practicing some more when Mrs. Armstrong called up: "Gentlemen, your cab is here!"

"Now who is she calling *gentlemen*?" chuckled Louis. "Two old rascals like you and me? *Heh, heh!* Grab your horn, Little Fred. Let's hit the city!"

Seven

Little Fred sat daydreaming in the cab's back seat while Louis sat up front chatting with the driver.

"Now, Pops," said the driver, "don't you know you're not supposed to put so much ochre into your red beans and rice? The key is to be subtle with the spices."

"Subtle, my black, er, *posterior*," said Louis. "Real New Orleans red beans and rice has. . . ."

I wonder if Mom ever sees me down here, thought the boy. *I wonder if she ever thinks about me. Do dead people remember the living?* She had died when Fred was nine. Although the raw ache in his heart had scabbed over during the past three years, he missed her more every day. To his relief, her memory was not fading. "Grow up to be a good man," she had said the morning of the day she died. "Be as good a man as your father and I'll be happy." *Is Dad happy? Is working and cooking dinner for us and reading at night enough for him?* Sometimes he worried about his father. *He doesn't laugh as much as he used to. I'd be in bed and from downstairs I'd hear the two of them laughing so hard. . . . I'd give ten years off the end of my life to talk to her for just ten minutes. Who wants to be old anyway?*

"You with us, Pops?" asked Louis.

"Yeah, I was just thinking."

The cab was on the Queensboro Bridge. A barge below was churning up the brown waters of the East River. A shimmering haze hung over Manhattan.

"It's going to be a steamer," said the cab driver.

Fifth Avenue was hopping, filled with business-men in hats and women in crisp summer dresses, all seemingly in a hurry. Soon they were in Greenwich Village, with Washington Arch straight ahead. The cab turned right, then made a left onto Seventh Avenue South, stopping in front of the red awning of the Village Vanguard. Louis and Fred stepped out, the boy making sure that his new trumpet was beneath his arm.

"Now that's too much of a tip, Pops," said the driver.

"No, it isn't," said Louis. "I've been very lucky in this world and I like to spread a little luck around."

"God bless you, Pops!" The cab blended into the traffic and was gone.

Louis led the way down a narrow staircase into the basement jazz club. All was dark and quiet and cool. Gazing about, Fred saw that the Vanguard was shaped like a red-carpeted funnel, with the stage at the spout. Long red-cushioned couches ran the length of both sides of the room and the walls were covered with photographs of the great musicians who had played there: Bill Evans, John Coltrane, Sonny Rollins, Thelonious Monk, Charles Mingus, Art Blakey, Horace Silver, Hank Mobley, Kenny Dorham, Sidney Bechet, and Louis Armstrong.

"Pops!" A small man with bright eyes rushed out of nowhere to hug Louis.

"Max!" boomed Louis. "The man who gives me honest employment, keeping me off the streets, *heh, heh!* Let me introduce you two rascals: Fred, this is the owner of this fine establishment, Mr. Max. And Max, this is my dear friend, Fred."

"Nice to meet you, sir," said Fred.

Max wrapped an arm around the boy. "Mutual, kid. You've nabbed a front row table tonight. Louis, naturally the place is going to be packed. Guess who called for tickets right after we hung up yesterday? Langston. I think I'll seat him with you, Fred."

The men retired to a corner to talk business.

Fred climbed up on the stage. For a moment he tried to picture himself playing his horn in front of a packed house, but the thought terrified him. *Every eyeball would be on me!* Sitting behind the drumkit, he gently swept the brushes across the snare. Then he sat down behind the piano and picked out *The Battle Hymn of the Republic* with one hand.

"Louis, do you mind if I take a walk over to Washington Square? I won't be gone long."

"Sure, Pops," said Louis. "I'll watch over your horn to make sure Max here doesn't pawn it."

Fred climbed up the dark staircase into August sunshine. Crossing Seventh Avenue, he strolled down sleepy, shady West 11th Street. His mother had loved Greenwich Village and countless times the two of them had explored its narrow streets, browsed in its art galleries, enjoyed Italian ices in its outdoor cafes.

As he turned onto Fifth Avenue, organ music poured from the open doors and windows of an ivy-shrouded stone church. Two lovely young mothers pushing strollers swept past. A bearded artist stood at the corner of 10th Street, dabbing green onto his canvas, a painting of the church. Up ahead loomed Washington Arch, the end of Fifth Avenue and gateway to Washington Square Park.

The park was filled with shade and people. Finding a bench by the stone chess tables, Fred closed his eyes, listening to the sounds of this summer afternoon in the city: the wild laughter of running leaping laughing children; automobile horns; a distant siren; the voices of two old men playing chess; the call of the park's balloonman; dogs barking. Somewhere nearby hamburgers were sizzling.

He thought of all the hours he had spent on park benches with his mother. Central Park, Union Square, Madison Square, Battery Park, and Washington Square. His mother had loved sitting on park benches with her son. "Watching people is better than the movies," she would say. "Plus, there's no sunshine or fresh air in a movie theater." Although he had also enjoyed running and leaping, in time Fred, too, grew to love the simple act of sitting outdoors and watching people. *I just liked being with her*, he thought. *It didn't matter what we were doing. Just being with her was enough.*

"Pardon me, kid," said a voice. "Do you have a quarter for a cup of coffee?"

Fred opened his eyes. A bewhiskered old man smelling of liquor stood weaving in front of him.

"Yeah, I think so," he said, reaching into his pocket. *Poor old guy. Man, you can really see the dirt in the creases of white people's skin.* "Here you go, sir."

The old man sat down on the bench beside him. "Name's Jim," he said, reaching out to shake Fred's hand. "Thank you kindly."

"Sure." *I just wanted to be left alone. . . .*

A coughing fit shook the old man's spindly frame. "Saw Teddy Roosevelt walk through this park," he said once he had caught his breath. "It was after he was president. He was all by himself—no bodyguards. Teddy didn't need no bodyguards. He died in 1919. This must've been 1916 or so."

Did you bum a quarter off Teddy, too? "Really?"

"Yup. I talked to him, too, but I forget what we talked about. I was just a kid." Warm boozy breath blew into Fred's face. "I wasn't always an old drunk, you know."

Gee, I figured you were born drunk with whiskers. "You don't seem that drunk to me."

"Well, I am. I think Teddy enjoyed a drink now and then, too. Think I read that somewhere. For your quarter, here's a story: Teddy had a long speech all written out on a whole lot of paper—fifty sheets or more. This was in 1912, after he was president, when he was running again for the Bull Moose Party. But at the last minute he decided to wing it, just talk off the top of his head. So he folded up the speech, over and over, and put it in his shirt pocket. Now while he was talking off the top of his head—he was speaking out doors, I think it was in Milwaukee—an assassin took a shot at old Ted. But guess what?"

This guy's interesting. "What?"

"All that folded up paper slowed down the bullet.

Old Teddy only suffered a flesh wound. The bullet would've killed him if the paper hadn't been there!"

"Is that a true story?"

The old man raised both hands to the sky. "My hands to God. Ah, you're a good kid. I can tell. I don't mean to frighten you. I'm gonna leave now. Thanks for the quarter. Here, let's shake." His hand felt warm and dry. "God bless you, kid." Unsteadily, he wandered off across the park.

I wonder if my grandfather was like that. Maybe that's why Dad's face gets so tight when he talks about his father. Or alcohol.

On Bleecker Street Fred found an old bookstore where he and his mother would browse. The same woman sat behind the same cash register, with the same glasses perched above her forehead. But other things were not the same. *Why do bookstores and sidewalks and park benches stay the same—but people die and are gone for good? Why can't people last as long as park benches?*

"Can I help you?" asked the woman in a tone that actually demanded: *Don't steal anything from my store, kid.*

"No," said Fred. "Thanks."

He took his time walking back to the Vanguard.

Eight

Louis and Fred ate dinner at an outdoor café on Thompson Street. Many of the men and women rushing home from work recognized the old musician, asking for his autograph. Patiently, Louis put his fork aside and signed their offered business cards and scraps of paper.

"Man, this place cooks up that good old New Orleans red beans and rice the way my mama—God rest her soul—used to," said Louis. A soft breeze ruffled the sleeves of his sports shirt. "We were in such a hurry to split that I forgot my suit for tonight. While you were out strolling, Miss Lucille—none too happy, I might add—had to drive it in for me."

Little Fred dug into his red beans and rice. *I'm beginning to like this stuff.* "Is she coming to the show tonight?"

"Naw. She's seen enough of my shows to last a turtle's age. She just wants to take a long bath and lie in bed and read." Louis chuckled. "Sounds pretty nice, too. No, you'll be sitting at the front table with an old friend of mine, Mr. Langston Hughes."

Fred couldn't believe his ears. "You mean the poet?"

"The same."

"Mr. Kendall, my English teacher, had us reading his poetry all the time. He tried to get Mr. Hughes to speak to our class but he was out of the country."

Louis shoveled in another heaping pile of red beans. "*Mmmmmmmm . . .* that's right. He just arrived home from Paris last week."

Remember that poem about the dream exploding? I wonder what a poet acts like? What do you say to a poet? Too bad Mr. Kendall won't be here tonight.

Back at the Vanguard the line of fans stretched up Seventh Avenue. Louis spent at least half an hour shaking hands, slapping backs, kissing cheeks, greeting old friends. "Thanks for coming out tonight, folks! I know there's a real fine episode of *Gunsmoke* on tonight, too, *heh, heh,* so I really appreciate it!"

"We love you, Pops!" a voice called.

"Right back at ya!" growled Louis.

Downstairs the club was quiet and cool. A moon-faced bald man took a clarinet out of his mouth. "Fred, my man!" he said.

"Hey, Barney."

45

A tall man with sleepy eyes named Trummy put down his trombone. "Want to jam with us, Freddieboy?" he asked.

Arvell, a tall, gentle soul, played a few runs on his bass. "Pops was flashing around your new horn. Pretty hip. How 'bout showing us what you can do with that thing?"

"Yeah, let's do it!" said Billy, seated at his piano.

An older man named Barrett—the only white musician in the band—sat behind his drum kit, twirling his sticks. "Well, *I'm* ready."

Now why doesn't this make me nervous? Grabbing his horn, Fred leapt up on the small stage. Barney played a few runs on his clarinet. "How about *Potato Head Blues*?" he suggested.

"Naw, something easier," said Fred. "I always fall apart on that one."

Louis, speaking with Max at the bar, laughed. "Ain't *that* the truth, Pops!"

Fred thought for a moment. "Let's play *Struttin' With Some Barbecue*. Louis and I have been practicing it."

Arvell counted off and in a moment Fred was launched into his favorite world: the world of playing improvised music with other musicians. Sure, practicing in his room was fun, but this was *it*, the real deal.

"It's like swimming," Louis had once said, "and the

other musicians are the water."

Concentrating, Fred negotiated all the changes at the correct moments, but somehow the music dragged. "*Let go*," mouthed Arvell. "*Just let go!*" Taking a deep breath, the boy closed his eyes and did just that.

"To me," Louis had once said, "the best times in music are when I'm not playing a trumpet—but when I'm playing *me*. Keep on practicing, Pops, and one day you'll know what I'm talking about."

At this moment the boy knew.

"That sure was swinging, Fred!" said Arvell as the last note faded away.

"Tasty," said Trummy.

"Quite fine," said Billy.

"Not bad at all," said Barney.

"*Whoooooeeee!*" said Louis. "For a few moments you left the trumpet behind, didn't you? You were playing *yourself*."

Smiling, Fred nodded. *Man, that felt incredible!*

"Superb," said a gray-haired man standing by the stairs. "Your tone reminds me of Clifford Brown's."

Rushing over, Louis embraced the man. "Well, well, well, what *do* you say, Brother Langston! You're looking mighty sleek for an old fella!"

"I'm two years younger than your old self."

The musicians put down their instruments and embraced the poet. Feeling shy, Fred hung back. Louis waved him over. "Come on, Pops!"

What do I say to a poet? "Hello, sir."

Langston Hughes held Fred's hands in both of his. "I guess gray hair confers upon me instant *sir*hood. Fine to meet you, son. Just call me *Langston*."

That was easy.

Max rushed over. "I'm opening the doors upstairs, gentlemen. Louis, get thee and the All Stars backstage. Are you hungry? There's some red beans and rice heating up back there. Langston, you and Fred have this table right in front."

"Don't you two be hurling no rotten fruit or dead cats up here tonight, y'hear?" said Louis with a wink. "Let's go, brothers."

Fred and the poet sat down. *I have no idea what to say.* Luckily, Langston spoke first: "I knew your mother, Fred."

"You did?" *I didn't know that.*

"Yes, indeed. Every spring she asked me to speak to her poetry classes at City College. One time I recall you were an infant in a carriage in the back of the classroom."

"She used to tell me that sometimes I'd wake up screaming."

"Not that day. Perhaps my presentation sent you to sleep—although I do recall a *malodorous* incident, shall we say."

Vocabulary word from last year . . . means bad smell-ing. Little Fred laughed.

"Your mother was a fine woman—a leader in our community and a superb teacher. She affected many young lives with her work. You probably don't remember, but I attended her funeral."

The boy stared at the table. His memory of that day was in slow-motion and black-and-white. *Change the subject,* he thought. "We studied some of your poems last year in my English class."

A crowd had assembled around the Vanguard's bar and people were now beginning to fill the tables. A pretty waitress brought the poet a lemonade and Fred a ginger ale. "Compliments of Mr. Satchmo," she said.

"Did you have any favorites?" asked Langston after thanking the waitress.

"Yeah. I loved the one about the college student who's the only black guy in his class. He's asked to write an essay."

"That's *Theme for English B.* I like that one myself. What did you like about it?"

"I don't know. I could just picture the guy sitting alone in his room trying to make his teacher know what it feels like to be him." *Am I sounding like an idiot?* "I also like how he gets records for Christmas presents. I do, too."

"*Bessie, bop, or Bach*," quoted the poet. "Any other of my poems that struck a chord?"

Fred sipped his ginger ale. "I really liked the one about the dream exploding."

"*A Dream Deferred*," said Langston.

"That's right. We didn't know what *deferred* meant, but our teacher Mr. Kendall made us look it up in the dictionary."

Japanese tourists, their cameras across their chests, sat at the tables surrounding Fred and Langston. In their rapid fire conversation, the word *Satchmo* kept popping up.

Langston smiled. "And how did that poem hit you?"

Fred took a deep breath. *Please sound almost intelligent.* "I *think* you're saying that if black folks don't get their share soon that . . . I don't know . . . that we're going to explode and just grab our share."

"You're exactly right, Fred. That poem is meant to be a warning—not necessarily a prediction. Let's pray to God that it never comes to violence—to an explosion. But I have to say that Dr. Martin Luther King and many young people not much older than you are beginning to stir things up down South—and they're dedicated to the idea of *non*violence. Gandhi called it *soul force*—to fight your enemy with the strength of your soul, your *being*, instead of with your fists—or a gun. Gandhi influenced an American philosopher named A. J. Muste and Mr. Muste has influenced Dr. King."

I don't think I understand, thought Little Fred. *Ask Dad or Louis about it.*

Suddenly Max was standing on the stage, clearing his throat, announcing Louis. *Good! Now I can relax my brain. Hope I didn't sound too stupid.* Fred glanced about. Black, white, Asian, Hispanic folks were now crammed into every nook and corner of the dark club. "Here he is!" said Max. "The one—the only—*Louis Armstrong!*"

Looking clean and sharp in a white suit, a red carnation in the lapel, Louis led his All Stars onto the Vanguard's stage. "Thank you very much, ladies and gentlemen," he said in his deep growl of a voice. "One—two—three—*four!*"

Man! Fred felt blown back by the sound, the sweep, the sheer *attack* of Louis' trumpet. It was a sound, as bright as sunshine, that he could physically *feel* in his chest and throat. *Get used to it: You will never be able to play like this. But that's all right. No one else can either. You'll just have to find your own sound. Whatever it is.*

Song followed song—*Royal Garden Blues; Tin Roof Blues; Black and Blue; Stardust; All of Me; Potato Head Blues; Twelfth Street Rag*—and the band swung each note with such joy that the Japanese tourists flung off their cameras and began to dance around their tables.

"Solid!" roared Louis over the scream of Barney's clarinet. Yet in a few minutes the *West End Blues* was played with such tender soul that a woman sighed as Louis' last note faded away.

Two hours later, awash in applause and sweat, Louis bowed and wished good night to the people. "God bless you, folks! Thanks for coming out tonight." Langston and Fred rushed backstage, where Louis hugged them both. "Whew!" he cried. "What would this world be without poetry and music? *Nothing*—that's what!"

It was well past midnight as Louis, Langston, Max and Fred stood on the sidewalk in front of the Vanguard, the city steamy and silent around them. Barney, Trummy, Arvell, Billy and Barrett had already packed up their instruments and headed uptown for a jam session in Harlem.

"Don't you want to go, too, Pops?" asked Langston.

"No, man. I'm bushed. This old dog needs his rest," said Louis.

The poet shook Fred's hand. "Was a pleasure meeting you, Fred. Hope to see you again. In the meantime keep playing that horn. I liked what I heard."

"So did I," said Max. "Keep on playing, kid, and pretty soon you can jump up onstage with Pops."

Louis beamed with pride. "Anytime you want, Little Fred, just let me know."

Are they kidding me? Fred wasn't sure. He only knew that the idea of standing onstage in front of an audience filled him with throat-grabbing fear.

Exhausted, he fell asleep on the cab ride home to Queens. He was vaguely aware of his father carrying him upstairs to bed.

"Dad?"

"Hmm?"

"Did I thank Louis?"

"Yes. Your eyes were closed, but you thanked him."

"Dad?"

"I'm still here, son."

"I didn't know Langston Hughes was at Mom's funeral."

"He was. Your mother was admired and respected by many people. Why she married a schmoe like me I'll never know."

"'Cause you're a good guy, that's why."

"Thanks—I take after my son. Good night, Fred. I love you."

"Love you too, Dad."

Nine

Ice cream cones in hand, three boys sat in the park across the street from Fat Pete's. The setting sun was painting the sky an eerie orange.

"Man, this ice cream is worth the crack on the head I'm going to get from my mama," said Steve.

"What are you talking about?" asked Fred.

"The dollar that paid for these babies was meant for a haircut. Tonight's the night Doc stays open 'til nine."

"Aaaaah!" Mark and Fred shoved their friend, nearly toppling his cone.

"Cut it out, man!" said Steve. "I want to at least enjoy my ice cream before getting whupped for it."

"Don't worry," said Fred. "My dad's having dinner with Louis tonight so the house is empty. Come on over and I'll cut your hair with the electric shears he uses on me."

"No funny business," said Steve.

Fred raised his hand. "Word of honor. You won't look any uglier than you normally do."

A neighbor strolled out to wax his car. Whistling, he placed his transistor radio on the car's roof. The Drifters were singing *Save the Last Dance for Me*.

"Bust me all you want," said Steve, "but you've never seen my mama mad. She scares me, man!"

At least you have a mother to be scared of, thought Fred.

"Ah, my mom's a softie," said Mark. "It's my dad I'm afraid of. When I get him really mad he makes like he's going to undo his belt to whip me."

Dad's never laid a hand on me. "Does he?" asked Fred.

"Naw—just reaching for the belt is enough for me. You should see his face when he's really mad. It's like Lon Chaney when he's changing into the Wolf Man."

The evening was darkening. Two hot rods tore off down the street. Mrs. Fontaine was calling for her cats. Fred swatted the air with his hand. "Ah, your parents are about as frightening as Minnie Mouse. What a bunch of old ladies I hang around with."

"Aren't you afraid of your old man?" asked Mark. "He's a big guy."

"Of course not. He's my dad. What's to be scared of?"

"You gotta admit," said Steve, "that Mr. B. is pretty cool."

"All right then," said Mark. "If it's not your old man, what *does* scare you?"

Fred thought for a moment. "Honest?" His friends nodded. "Well, it's the thought of playing my trumpet in front of an audience. I can't even *think* about it without feeling like I'm going to puke."

"What are you talking about?" said Mark. "You always play those concerts with the school band and you blow real fine every time. Me and Stevie are proud to know you."

Is he busting my chops again? Doesn't seem to be. I think he really means it.

As the boys talked, they watched two pretty girls step off the bus across the street. No one commented.

"Naw," said Fred, "that's easy *oom-pa-pa* stuff. You learn that music once and you can play it forever. No, I'm talking about playing *jazz*."

"What's so hard about it?" asked Steve. "It's only music."

"Man!" said Fred. "You know how to pull a sly one over on your mama, but you know *nothing* about jazz."

"So explain yourself, Professor Bradley," said Mark.

"Well. . . ." *Don't sound full of yourself.* ". . . with jazz you're making it up as you go along. It's not written down like the school band's music. You're creating it on the spot, as you play. And if your mind messes up for even a *second* it's a disaster. Everything falls apart."

"You mean on my dad's Miles records, all of them musicians are making it up as they go along?" asked Mark.

"Yup."

"How about Duke?"

"Well, Duke is a composer so a lot of his music is written down. But Louis says that Duke always leaves plenty of room for his musicians to be creative. *Improvising*, it's called."

A pretty woman pushing a baby carriage strolled past.

"So when you play with Louis, are you improvising?" asked Steve.

"Yeah, but Louis takes it slow with me. Like if Don Newcombe was pitching to you, he'd probably give you a break because you're a kid. He wouldn't try to blow it by you. But if I ever climb up onstage with Louis, it'll be ninety miles per hour fastballs every time—and I'm not sure I'm ready for that."

Standing, Mark sunk his napkin in a trashcan. "Two points, boys. Now that you mention it, Trumpetboy, playing jazz sounds scarier than my old man and Stevie's mama put together. I'm glad I'm not you."

"Thanks. You want to head over to my house for Stevie's haircut? I think there's more ice cream in the freezer."

"Let's go, man!"

Mick Carlon

The rubber soles of their P.F Flyers slapping against the pavement, the three boys shot off toward Little Fred's house.

Ten

While the boys ran, two men sat on a park bench on the Brooklyn side of the East River. As the sunset painted the river lava-red, the skyscrapers beyond were flickering on their first evening lights.

"Sometimes it's like you died, too," said Louis.

Big Fred shook his head as if he'd been slapped. "Now that's not fair, Pops. My whole life is wrapped up in Fred. If *that's* being d—"

"We're not talking here about your talents as a father," said Louis. "Man, I'd've given *anything* to have a father like you—and that's the truth. What we're talking about here is *you*, Fred. *Your* life. Only six more years and Fred's in college, off living *his* life. What're you going to be doing? Reading even more newspapers?"

Big Fred watched a helicopter land on Roosevelt Island. *They all think he's so genial*, he thought, *always laughing and joking. They don't know the real Louis Armstrong. Man, he's as serious as life itself.*

Whipping out a white handkerchief, Louis mopped his forehead. "You know I loved Lorraine like a daughter—but she's *gone*, Fred. She's gone, God rest her. And you're still here, as stubborn as ever."

Big Fred stood up. "Oh, thanks for the news, Pops. And here I was thinking she'd gone out for some milk and gotten lost." *Keep your voice under control!* Crisping his fingers through a chain-link fence by the river's edge, he watched a tugboat chug past.

The dear boy needs a wake-up call, thought Louis. *But did I go too far?* For a long while the two men were silent, both watching the river and the city beyond. Finally, Louis said, "Did I ever tell you what I said to the pope?"

The tears on Big Fred's face were drying. "No, what?" Smiling in spite of himself, he walked back to his friend.

"So I'm standing there at the Vatican with Lucille and the pope says, 'Do you and Mrs. Armstrong have any children?' And I say: 'No, Your Excellency, but we sure do enjoy trying every night!' *Heh heh heh!*"

Big Fred reached out for the old musician's hand. "I'm sorry, Pops. I didn't mean to lose my temper."

"Maybe you should lose it more. Sweet Lorraine sure could lose hers, if you recall."

Shaking his head, Big Fred smiled. "Can't deny it." A hawk was circling one of the towers of the 59th Street Bridge. "Alright—so tell me about her."

Rubbing his hands together, Louis grinned. "Now we're talking! Her name is Sarah Ann Fagan and man, she sings with some soul. She's a lovely creature but a downhome gal, too. Nothing stuck-uppity about her, no sir! When the show's over she slips into some jeans and a t-shirt and says, *Howdydo!*"

"What does she want with a guy who works in a plant by the East River?"

"What the gal is looking for is a sincere man with a good heart. 'He doesn't have to be as good looking as you, Pops,' she said. And you, my stubborn son, definitely fit the bill!"

The helicopter rose over Roosevelt Island, darting down toward the Battery.

"Alright," said Big Fred. "You win. What's her phone number?"

Louis let out a whoop. "No, siree, *you're* the winner—which you will realize the second you lay eyes on this fine, sweet gal!"

Eleven

Fred skidded across the grass. A baseball lay nestled in the pocket of his mitt.

"I was robbed!" cried Steve.

"Hey, Trumpetboy can catch, too," said Mark.

The bells of a Good Humor truck announced a break in their homerun derby contest. Ice cream bars in hand, the three boys relaxed in the shade. "Boys!" called old Mrs. Fontaine from across the street.

"Ma'am?" said Mark.

"Have you seen my Queenie?" she asked.

"Is that the red one?"

"Yes," said the old woman. "I haven't seen her all morning."

"We haven't seen her, ma'am," said Fred, "but we'll keep our eyes peeled."

"Thank you, boys," said Mrs. Fontaine, tottering back to her front porch.

"How many cats does she have?" asked Steve.

"I don't know," said Mark, "but I was in her house when I had that paper route and they were *all* over the place. I was sneezing in no time."

For a long time the three friends, all sprawled in the grass, were quiet, each gazing up at the sky.

"Back to school next week," said Fred.

"Shut up," said Steve. "Don't remind me. Why can't they just leave us alone? Man, all I want to do is hang out in our park and play ball. School gets in the way!"

"Seventh grade," said Fred. "We're getting up there."

"Just six more years of school," said Steve, "and we're *done.*"

"What are you—the village idiot?" snapped Mark. "My dad says I'm going to City College so I can do better than he's done. He socks away money from his pay every week for me. So does my mom."

"I wasn't counting college," mumbled Steve.

"How about you, Trumpetboy?" asked Mark. "You going to Trumpet University or what?"

His eyes closed, Fred could still see the shadows of swaying branches above him. "I don't know. My dad keeps hinting about going to college to be a dentist, but I'm not interested. I want to play music for a living. I guess I could shoot for Julliard, but then I think how Louis never went to college."

"What does Louis say about it?" asked Steve.

"I've never asked him."

Mark snickered. "Kind of hard to earn your living playing music when you're terrified of the audience, isn't it? Unless, of course, the people are paying to see you puke!"

For a second Fred was furious. *But he's right. . . .* "Yeah, well, I guess I have to get over that."

Steve yawned. "I just hope I like my job more than my dad does. The poor guy's worn *out* when he gets home."

"Mine, too," said Fred, drifting off. His friends' voices melted away as he thought of his father, home from work, washing his hands at the kitchen sink before cooking dinner. The few times Fred had tried surprising his father with dinner had been disasters. One evening in May the smoke had been so dense that old Mrs. Washington next door had called the fire department. "No more surprises, son," his father had said.

But Little Fred, before starting his homework, always washed and dried the pots and pans and dishes. He also pitched in by vacuuming the house—one room a day—and by keeping his room clean.

"I don't know what I'd do without your help," Big Fred had said just last night. "But put down that dish towel and let's play some catch before it's too dark."

"Hey!" Mark yelled in his ear. *"Wake up, Trumpet-boy!"*

Startled, Fred sat up. "Sorry—guess I fell asleep."

His friends laughed. "Come on," said Steve. "It's my turn at bat. Do you want to pitch or play the outfield?"

"I'll take the outfield," said Fred, jogging out into left. His hands on his knees, he called, "Come on, Markus! No batter up there!"

Crash! Steve hit one sweet and solid. Pivoting, Fred turned and dashed deeper and deeper, closer to 110th Street. *Watch the street*, he told himself. *No running out there.*

Screetch! A blue automobile slammed to a stop. The lady behind the wheel—gray-haired, grandmotherly, and white—glared at the black boy standing on the grass. "Watch where you're going, you stupid nigger! I could've killed you!" After another glare, she drove off.

Stunned, Little Fred watched the car disappear. In a flash Steve and Mark were beside him.

"Did you *hear* that witch?" said Mark.

"Did you get her license plate number?" asked Steve.

"What's he going to do?" asked Mark. "Call the cops because some white woman called him a *nigger*? Use your head!"

Dad said it would happen one day. Failing to push back the tears, Fred wiped his arm across his eyes.

"I know it hurts, man," said Mark. "My mama's old butcher called me that word once. That's why my mama has a new butcher."

He said it would happen. And he was right.

"Mister Harrington called me it once," said Steve.

"That pimply shop teacher?" asked Mark.

What did I do to deserve that?

"Yeah. He whispered it to me last winter: 'If you break one more jigsaw, you little nigger, I'll break your fingers.'"

She doesn't know me.

"What did you do?" asked Fred, walking in toward the backstop behind home plate.

Steve looked down at his sneakers. "Nothing. Why bother?"

SHE DOESN'T KNOW ME!

Picking up Steve's 32 ounce Willie Mays Louisville Slugger, Fred swung wildly at one of the backstop's metal posts. *Crack!* A splinter of wood flew past Mark's head.

"Watch out!"

Crack! A chunk of bat sailed off, followed by another, and another, and another. Steve and Mark shielded their heads with their arms. In a few moments only a small piece of the handle was left in Fred's hands.

Panting wildly, feeling as though he'd just awakened from an exhausting dream, he doubled over, his hands on his knees.

What just happened?

"Man!" said Steve. "That was out of control!"

Mark laid his hand on Fred's shoulder. "You okay, man?"

Without warning, Fred vomited. "Woah!" said Mark. "Watch the sneakers!" *Why did that happen?* His legs trembled. *Why?* Wiping his mouth with his sleeve, he said, "Yeah, I'm okay. I'm sorry. Are you guys alright? You didn't get hit, did you?"

Mark grinned. "By baseball bat—or puke?"

Steve dashed left, then right. "Naw, I was dodging them wooden bullets like Batman! Didn't you see me?"

Mark's hand was still on his friend's shoulder. "You alright?"

"Yeah, I'm fine. I guess it had to happen sometime." Fred picked up his glove. "I think I'm going to go home. I just want to be alone," he lied.

"You still want to go swimming this afternoon?"

"I don't know. Maybe."

"Steve and I will be at the pool around two. Okay?"

What just happened? "Yeah. Okay. Hey, I'll pay for your bat, Steve."

"Whenever, Fred. No trouble."

"I'm sorry." Fred felt his feet moving. "See you guys."

The two boys watched their friend walk away. "It never bothered me that much," said Steve. "I just shrugged it off. How about you?"

Mark gave a last wave to his friend. "Naw—it bothered me just as bad. I'm just a better actor than our Trumpetboy."

Twelve

I don't want to bug Dad at work, Fred thought, *and he won't be home until at least six.* He walked past his own house. Five minutes later he was knocking on his friend's screen door. "Louis?" he called. "Louis?"

"Come on in, Pops!" growled that familiar voice. "I'm up in the den!"

Louis was sitting at his desk, his eyeglasses balanced on the tip of his nose. Dressed in blue Bermuda shorts, a Fats Waller t-shirt, white socks and tan sandals, he was busy creating a collage for yet another reel-to-reel tape box.

"Fred, my man! Great to see you. Grab a seat, Pops." The boy plopped down on the den's comfortable old couch. "I'll be finished here in a second or five. Miss Lucille is out food shopping. She should be home soon. Are you hungry?"

"No, thanks."

Something in the boy's voice made Louis look up. "You okay?" he asked.

Against his will, the tears began to spill off Fred's face. He lowered his head and cried. Rushing over, Louis wrapped an arm around his friend. "What's wrong, son?"

Between sobs Fred told him. Louis was quiet for a long while. When the boy finally looked up, he could see that the old musician's eyes were also filled with tears. "I'm sorry," said Louis. "I'm so sorry."

"She doesn't even know me," said Fred. "She doesn't know my dad or my—"

Louis gently squeezed the boy's neck. "No, she doesn't. And that's what hurts, isn't it? That some ignorant old biddy can call you something so hateful—so wrong—when she *does not know you at all*." He sighed.

Fred was staring at the carpet. "Have you ever been called it?"

"Son, I've been called that word as many times as I have wrinkles on this old black face. Hurts every time. In fact, one Tuesday I was in Rome, meeting the pope—*because the pope wanted to meet old Pops*. Imagine that! Then, the following Tuesday, the band and I were in Connecticut, rushing to a one-nighter. We pulled over because I had to use the rest room—and the white owner of the gas station said, 'I don't allow no niggers to use my facilities.' In my own country! A *week* after I met the pope!"

The boy looked up. "It's just so wrong."

Louis closed his eyes. "A long time ago—I was about thirty years old—I returned to my hometown of New Orleans. Been away a good nine years or more. My boys and I were playing at a place called the Suburban Gardens—the first black band to ever do so—and, man, the place was *packed*.

"Now the joint, of course, was segregated, and that was bothering me no end. Our people had to stand outside, hoping to grab some of that good music from the open windows. They told me later that five thousand folks were inside the place—and over *ten thousand* black folks outside, standing right along the levee. I strolled outside before the show and saw many of the good folks I'd grown up with. They pounded my back and said, 'Blow that horn, Dipper!' (*Dipper* being my childhood nickname because of my rather large mouth, *heh, heh*). My God, was I a proud man that night!

"The show was being zoomed out on the radio, too. So a bit later I'm standing on the stage and the radio announcer—a squirrely looking white boy—was supposed to announce me and my band. But he kept looking at me while tugging on his collar. Finally, at the last moment, he approached the microphone, said, 'I can't announce this nigger man,' and stormed off.

71

"Can you imagine this? All of our people listening at home on their radios heard this hatred, as well as the ten thousand folks on the levee. So I turned to my boys, said, 'Give me a chord.' They gave me one that came close to shattering the windows and I stepped to the microphone and announced *myself*. I was told later that this was the first time a black man ever spoke on the radio down South."

The friends locked eyes.

"I'm sorry, son."

"It's okay. I'm feeling better."

Standing up, Louis walked slowly over to a closet. *He seems so tired sometimes. Where does his energy come from?* From inside he grabbed an old tarnished trumpet. "The Prince of Wales gave me this baby a long time ago. Doesn't look like much but it still wails. Want to play some music on it?"

Louis held out the old horn while picking up his own. Little Fred stood up.

"You see, Pops, the key to jazz is simply being *yourself*. You don't have to pound like old Louis, or like Diz, or sound mysterious and lonely like Miles. You simply have to find your *own* sound. Just be your fine Fred self. Blow on your horn what you're *feeling* that day. Maybe a pretty girl smiled at you this morning at Fat Pete's. So then play *that* warm feeling on your horn. Or maybe you whiffed four times in your baseball game. Well, then, play *those* low-down blues and make them sound as sad and soulful as can be." The old man looked hard at the boy. "Or maybe an ignorant old soul who hasn't yet learned what life is about called you a hateful name. So play *that* pain and anger on your horn. Ready? One—two—three—*four!*"

Go! The two friends dove into the most scalding, ferocious music Little Fred had ever played. (*How long did it last?* he later asked himself). His eyes closed, he poured out his hurt in a harsh rush of notes that demanded release. Yet at the same moment he was also listening carefully to his friend. With each scream from Fred's trumpet, Louis answered musically with furious affirmation, *I know, I know, I know, I know. . . .* The two were literally communicating through music. As the duet began to wind down—an unearthly, yearning cry—Little Fred, exhausted, began to tremble. With a supreme effort, he held the last note until it faded away into the sound of children playing across the street.

The old man and the boy stared at one another, both astonished at the music they had just created. "*You're it!*" cried one of the children. Reaching for his handkerchief, Louis began mopping his brow.

"Pops," he said, "you are one true musician."

Thirteen

That evening Little Fred cooked dinner—tuna fish, macaroni and cheese, and peas—and even volunteered to clean up while his father read the evening newspapers.

"Son, you are awfully quiet in there," Big Fred called from the living room. "Everything alright?"

"Yeah, Dad, I'm fine."

His father appeared in the kitchen doorway. "The news today is just getting me down. Want to play catch?"

"No, thanks."

Joking, Big Fred placed a hand on his son's forehead. "How high's the fever? Should I call Doctor Tuttle?" Suddenly, his son's story began to tumble out in a torrent of words. "Woah, son. Let's sit down. Now *slow* down. I'm listening."

Big Fred didn't take his eyes from his son's eyes

as Fred told every detail. *Don't cry*, the boy told himself. *Dad doesn't need to see you cry. Keep it in.* Soon the story was told. Big Fred sighed. Little Fred felt a warm, rough hand covering his own. "I'm so sorry, son. Even though I told you to prepare yourself for this, it doesn't make it any easier to take. Believe me. I know."

"But it would be harder now if you hadn't warned me. Really."

Big Fred sighed. "I don't know what to tell you. Sadly, it's part of the world we live in. You and me alone can't make hatred go away. Hatred is reality. But you and me can never become haters ourselves. That would be the tragedy. Your mother wouldn't want that."

"I know. But I was so mad it was scary. I didn't know what I was doing, but I smashed Steve's Willie Mays bat to splinters. And all the time I wanted to be hitting that old woman right in the face."

Big Fred was silent for a moment. "Now you know that's not right."

"Of course I do. I would never hurt some stupid old woman—but I sure hurt that old bat. Pieces were flying everywhere. Steve and Mark had to duck."

"Were they hurt?"

Little Fred suddenly realized: *I could have injured my friends. I didn't even think about them. I was so mad*

75

I forgot about my friends. He looked down at his hands. "No, no one was hurt."

"Luckily." Standing up, Big Fred said, "It goes without saying that you're going to buy Steven a new bat. Want a root beer? I'm thirsty."

"Sure."

They drank their root beers cold from the can, neither saying a word. Big Fred was looking out the kitchen window at the setting sun. "Did I ever tell you about my Army friend Anthony?" he asked. Little Fred shook his head. "He was a white guy from New Hampshire and we were both stationed in Berlin, Germany after the war ended. He was a grunt soldier and I was responsible for keeping the jeeps on the base in working order. But for some reason we became friends. He liked jazz, too, and we swapped stories of the bands we'd seen. He was a Lester Young fanatic.

"Anyways, I've told you how the Army was segregated—separate barracks, separate mess quarters and the like. Well, Anthony had a backbone and because we were friends he'd eat with us black soldiers in our mess hall. For several days no one seemed to care. But one evening this white captain—Martilla was his name—came strutting into our mess and chewed out Anthony for eating with us. 'What are you, soldier—a nigger lover?' I remember him saying."

Little Fred winced. His father noticed, but continued: "'You prefer eating with these monkeys rather than with your own?' He was really in old Anthony's face. 'Private Bradley is my friend,' Anthony replied. 'I enjoy his company and prefer to eat here.'

"Martilla had a fit and called in the MPs—military police—and they dragged Anthony out and threw him in the brig for the night. I remember seeing him the next morning, whistling and smiling. I was changing the oil on a general's jeep and he strolls up as cheerful as you please. 'See you tonight at chow, Fred,' he said.

"'Don't do nothing foolish now, Anthony,' I said, dropping my voice. 'That Martilla is one crazy mother and you don't know what he could do.'

"'Ah, he's done his worst,' my friend said and, sure enough, at chow time there he was, tray in hand, walking over to sit with me. But here comes Martilla, the MPs not far behind, just waiting for him to place that tray down. Now I could see Anthony's face working—*What should I do here?*—and then he winked at me, said, 'What the hell?' and slapped that tray down next to mine."

Little Fred had forgotten his troubles. "What happened?"

"Martilla gave the command, the MPs swooped down, and poor Anthony was dragged kicking and yelling out of the mess hall. 'I can eat with my friend if I choose! We're both *Americans* for God's sake!' he kept yelling over and over until his voice had disappeared.

"Captain Martilla strutted over to me, coughed up a lung cookie, and spat it on my food. 'Eat *that*, nigger,' he said—then walked cool as brass out of the mess hall. I had a fork in my hand and so help me I could've buried it in that fool's chest. But I didn't. I closed my eyes, counted to ten, and thought of my life ahead. If I had attacked that ignorant bigot, the Army would have locked me up for life, I never would have met your mother, and you wouldn't be here today." He looked deep into his son's eyes. "Sometimes a man has to take a deep breath, count to ten, and think of his future."

Little Fred nodded. *I know what he means.* "I understand. What happened to Anthony?"

"He was locked up for two weeks and then—I received a letter from him—they sent him to some battlefield to dig up the corpses of American soldiers that had been buried in a mass grave and put each one in a plastic bag."

"You're kidding, right?"

"No."

"Where is he now?"

The kitchen was shadowy in the fading sunlight. Big Fred stood and switched on a light. "I have no idea. That's the first and last letter I received from him. Every now and again I'll call a telephone operator in Nashua, New Hampshire to ask if there's a number for Anthony Giggliotti, but there never is."

He's such a thoughtful boy, Big Fred thought. *God, please bless and protect my child. Let him lead a good and loving life. Let him live to be a great-grandfather. Amen. Should I tell him? No. He's suffered enough for today. I won't tell him yet. She sure sounded nice on the phone.*

Big Fred stood up. "Nothing against your dinner, son, it was fine—but I'm in the mood for some ice cream. Are you up for a walk to Fat Pete's? My treat."

Smiling, the boy nodded. "You know what Louis said about that old lady?" he asked.

"What?"

"That she just hasn't learned yet what life is all about."

Big Fred hugged his son. "I'd say that's right. But I'm proud to say that my son is learning more and more every day."

Fourteen

Climbing a steep staircase, father and son emerged on the wooden pedestrian pathway of the Brooklyn Bridge. Little Fred breathed in deeply. A late August breeze was sweeping off the river. Tiny white lights illuminated the bridge's cables while Manhattan prepared itself for the Saturday night ahead.

Stopping, they leaned against a railing and stared at the city. One lone tugboat was chugging up the dark waters of the East River. The sounds of cars and sirens sounded far-off, muffled. Above them soared the bridge's stone ramparts and its buzzing cables.

"At the end of the war," said Big Fred, "I was handed some free time so I traveled a bit. One afternoon in Paris I rented a bicycle and decided to ride out to Chartres to see its cathedral. I didn't make it that day, so I spent the night in a small country inn. But the next morning I was cycling through a field of wheat when up ahead I saw it: two stone spires sticking up from the roofs of a small market town. I couldn't believe that something so precious and beautiful had been spared by the Nazis. I spent the entire morning walking outside then inside the cathedral, exploring every corner. And you know what?"

"What?"

"It's no more beautiful than this bridge—and that's a fact."

As the sky grew darker, the city grew brighter.

"Have you ever heard of this singer?" asked Big Fred.

"Yup. There was an article about her in *Down Beat*—with a picture, too. She's really pretty." When his father had suggested going to the Village Vanguard to hear the singer Sarah Ann Fagan, Little Fred had checked out the club's ad in the *Times* and seen that a talented young trumpeter, Mark Wainwright, was in her band.

Big Fred cleared his throat. "There's, um, something I didn't tell you about tonight, son."

"What?"

"You see, Louis is trying to play matchmaker between me and this Sarah Ann. He gave me her phone number and she knows we're coming to the show tonight and, um, we might go out for coffee afterwards."

For a moment Little Fred was speechless. "But

you're too old for her," he finally said.

"What do you mean? She's twenty-nine years old. I'm not too old."

"But what are you—fifty?"

"Hey! Your old man isn't *that* old! I'm only thirty-eight. Give a dude a break."

Wait a minute. How do I feel about this? Dad might start dating someone.

"How about a reaction?"

Little Fred tried to smile. "It's just weird. That's all."

"It's really no big deal. We're just going to grab a cup of coffee. You're welcome to join us or you can go browse at Bleecker Bob's and pick out an album." Big Fred wrapped an arm around his son. "I'm sorry I didn't mention it sooner. I guess I didn't know how to bring it up."

"That's okay."

"Really?"

This time the smile was for real. "When she gets a good look at your old self, she'll probably be interested in *me*!"

"She'll make a fine looking daughter-in-law, that's for sure. Come on, let's go."

Once again a crowd stood waiting to descend the Vanguard's stairs to the club below. As father and son took their place in back of the line, a familiar voice called out, "*Hey, Fred!*"

Max, the club's owner, rushed up, out of breath. "What's my favorite young musician doing waiting in line?" Little Fred introduced Max to his father. "Your son has a gift," said Max with a wink, "and it's those gifted ones who always gouge me for the big bucks. So since tonight's show is on the house, remember this favor one day, Fred."

Max led them past the crowd—and a few grumbles—and down the stairs to a table beside the stage. The house-lights made the drum kit sparkle like a Christmas present. A quiet young man sat at the piano, tinkling various notes and chords.

"Louis told me the whole story," said Max to Big Fred. "She's backstage all nervous to meet you."

A look of disbelief crossed Big Fred's face. "You're kidding."

"No kidding," said Max. "I guess Louis really sold you. Well, enjoy the show, gentlemen."

Big Fred ordered two colas from a young waitress.

"Did you notice that?" asked Little Fred after the waitress had gone.

"What?"

"She was checking you out big time."

Shaking his head, Big Fred smiled. "When you're hot, you're hot."

Little Fred looked around. Once again a table was

crowded with Japanese tourists, their cameras around their necks. The young pianist stood, surveyed the crowd, then headed backstage. Big Fred nodded toward the tourists. "Look," he said quietly. "Fifteen years ago we were trying to kill each other and now we visit each others' countries and take pictures. Makes you realize how stupid war is."

"We read a World War I poem last week in Mr. Kendall's class," said Little Fred, "about two soldiers trying to kill each other across a field. I forget the poet's name but he began thinking how he and the other soldier, if there'd been no war, could have been two friends having a beer in a pub."

"Thomas Hardy wrote it," said Big Fred, smiling, as his son did a double-take. "Not bad for a guy who works for the electric company." He shrugged. "Hey, your mom made me read a lot of poetry."

Grinning, Little Fred asked the question he had asked dozens of times: "Did you ever kill anyone in the war, Dad?"

"No." Again a warm, gap-toothed smile. "But I peeled a lot of potatoes!"

Suddenly a tall young woman in a blue dress stood before them. "Good evening," she said into the microphone. "I'm Sarah Ann Fagan and this is my band." The same young pianist took his seat at the keyboard. A drummer and bassist, both in sharp blue suits, took their places behind their instruments. And Mark Wainwright, his golden trumpet almost brushing the carpet, stood in a dark corner of the stage, staring up at the lights. As Sarah Ann surveyed the crowd, it was clear that she was looking for someone. *She's beautiful*, Little Fred thought, immediately feeling guilty. *But not as beautiful as Mom.*

Her coffee-colored skin glowing beneath the lights, Sarah Ann closed her eyes and began to sing. It was *Stormy Weather*, a song Little Fred's mother had loved. With a gentle yet propulsive *whoosh*, the pianist, bassist, and drummer, on brushes, joined in. Opening her lovely eyes, the singer once again scanned the crowd. With a sudden start she laughed, making it part of the song. Right in front of her sat the person she'd been looking for. *She's looking at Dad!* Immediately, Big Fred picked up his cola, staring hard at the ice-cubes. Looking over, the singer winked at Little Fred. He winked back. *Man, I'm smooth!* Looking over, he saw that his father had found reasons to find his shoes fascinating.

The crowd applauded. Nodding, Sarah Ann strolled slowly away from the microphone as Mark Wainwright approached. *Look at him. He's not scared at all.* Little Fred was surprised at how young Wainwright was, no more than a boy in his blue suit and gleaming black shoes. Yet when he brought his horn to his lips and blew, Fred knew that he was in the presence of an artist whose skills and ideas were far above his own. Like a young ballplayer watching Willie Mays take batting practice, Little Fred studied the techniques of a total professional. As the show continued, every note from Wainwright's horn seemed to caress the singer's notes. When she sighed, his horn sighed. When she growled, his horn growled. He played with power but a quiet, subtle power—quite different from Louis' blasts of sunshine. Song followed song and as the last cymbal splash of the last number faded away, Sarah Ann smiled, stepped off the stage, and disappeared. The lights came up.

"The lady certainly can sing," said Big Fred, standing, "and your man Wainwright is a fine musician, too."

Max rushed up. "You two aren't leaving, are you? Sarah wanted to say hello backstage."

"Then I guess we're not leaving," said Big Fred.

Backstage was a shadowy room with several chairs and empty beer crates. Sarah Ann, flushed and even lovelier up close, sat on a crate fanning herself with a magazine. "Hello," she said, smiling shyly.

To Little Fred's surprise, his father walked right up and shook her hand. "How do you do, Miss Fagan. I'm Fred Bradley and this is my son, Fred."

"The two Freds," said the singer.

"Hi," said Little Fred. *Wow, she's pretty. Has a strong handshake, too.*

"Louis tells me you're quite the musician," said Sarah.

"Thanks." *I wish I was home watching* Gunsmoke *right now. I wish Dad was rubbing Mom's feet.*

"We enjoyed your show," said Big Fred. "You sing beautifully."

She actually looks embarrassed, thought Little Fred. *I have to admit—she smells good.*

Just then Mark Wainwright walked in. "Hey, Sarah, have you seen—? Oh, sorry. I didn't know you had guests."

Sarah handled the introductions. "And Fred here is one of Louis Armstrong's prize pupils."

Wainwright's eyes widened. "No kidding? Pops?" As the trumpeter guided Little Fred by the elbow to a far corner, Sarah and Big Fred began to quietly talk.

"I don't care how modern a cat might think he is," said Wainwright. "If he plays trumpet then he's playing some Pops. Louis is the source of the river, man. Is it true that he calls other people *Pops*, too?"

"Yup—even me." Although he was thrilled to be speaking to the young musician, Little Fred kept an eye on his father and Sarah. *He's leaning in a little close there. And look at her. She can't stop touching his arm. She is pretty, though. The poor guy needs more in his life than me and his newspapers. But what about Mom?* Naturally, he knew the answer, but to be once again reminded of it hurt beyond words: *Your mother is dead, boy, and she's never coming back. Dad knows it. Why don't you? Even if you live to be 110 you'll never see her again.*

Never.

Never.

Never.

"Hey, Earth to Fred," said Wainwright, snapping his fingers. "Where are you, man?"

He felt his father's hand on his shoulder. "He's in a nightclub near midnight and he's exhausted. Come on, son, let's go home." Big Fred shook Wainwright's hand. "Tonight was like hearing Sweets Edison playing behind Billie Holiday. Thank you." Wainwright beamed.

Sarah Ann's smile was sincere. "That's one of the nicest compliments I've ever been paid." On her tiptoes she kissed Big Fred on the cheek. "Thank you."

"You're very welcome. I'll call you." *What a smooth dog!* "Let's go, son."

A light drizzle was falling. Max, standing beneath his red awning, was chatting with Sarah's pianist and bassist. "Thanks for coming, you two."

"Thank you for the free ride," said Big Fred.

"No problem. Just remind your son when he's a hot-shot trumpeter that he owes me a free gig. Hey,

Little Fred, send my best to Pops."

"I will, Max. Night."

"Goodnight, good sirs both."

On the cab ride home both father and son were quiet. After washing his face and brushing his teeth, Little Fred said his prayers. As always, his first prayer was for his mother; his second prayer for his father; and his third prayer for Louis. *He flies so much, please watch over his airplanes.* Picking up his grandfather's battered old horn, he gently blew one of the phrases he had heard Mark Wainwright play that evening. *Sometimes I feel guilty for not playing this horn more. I should use it as much as the new one.* The notes, however, sounded forced, almost strangled. *Forget that.*

A knock on the door. Big Fred, out of the shower and in his plaid bathrobe, poked his head in the door. "That old devil sounds pretty sad," he said.

Little Fred placed his grandfather's horn on the night table. "You said it." Picking up his new horn, he played the same phrases. They sounded tight and crisp.

"Now that's more like it," said Big Fred, lying down on the floor, his hands behind his head. "So . . . how're you feeling?"

Little Fred put down the trumpet. "About what?"

"About the stock market. Come on, son. Let's talk."

"About what?"

Big Fred sighed. "About the fact that Louis has set me up with an attractive woman who seemed to like me and who I might ask out to dinner next week."

"That's fine. It doesn't bother me at all."

"Are you sure?"

He looked his father in the eye. "Dad, it's fine. Go out with her if you want. It doesn't bother me at all."

You had a streak going, boy. It's been years since you've lied to Dad. What were you? Five? Six? You broke his watch and blamed it on the cat. Remember how guilty you felt? You promised yourself that you'd never lie to him again. Too bad—the streak just ended.

Fifteen

Early September 1959. A cool evening, sweater weather, in the park across the street from Fat Pete's Ice Cream Parlor.

Holding his pistachio cone aloft, Louis cleared his throat. "Ha-*humph!* I'd like to announce a toast to a successful school year up ahead for my fine friend Fred."

Laughing, the two held their cones high. "Where are you going tomorrow?" asked Little Fred.

"Let's see: First we'll be playing Chicago, then it's a hop, skip, and a leap to Denver, Colorado and then all the way down the West Coast: Seattle, Portland, San Fran, the City of Angels, and San Diego. Then we'll be ske-daddling over to Honolulu—where Miss Lucille can work on her sun tan, *heh, heh*—and then it's on over to Japan, where those good people really love their jazz."

Man, I'd love to go with Louis and the All Stars sometime. The furthest from Queens I've ever been is Coney Island!

"When will you be home?"

"The second week of November—right after you receive your first report card, if I'm not mistaken." Louis winked. "Now your dad and I are two sneaky rascals and we've been conspiring behind your back, Pops."

"Yeah?" *What's he going to say?*

"The All Stars and I are scheduled to play in Nashville, Tennessee on November 21 or 22. I forget which. If you, my friend, make the honor roll for the first term, then you can travel on down with us."

Fred leapt off the bench. "You're kidding!"

"Nosiree. Miss Lucille just wants to stay home and start cooking up all that good food for Thanksgiving, so she suggested I take you. I talked it over with your dad and he suggested this might be a good way to get you working a tad harder on your math. So, is it a deal?"

Fred slapped Louis' outstretched palm. "It's a deal! I'm going to ace every math quiz old Mr. Perfito throws at me!"

"There's the spirit. Hey, why not bring down your horn to Tennessee and blow some fine music on stage with us? I think you're ready, Fred. I wasn't blowing so fine when *I* was twelve."

Oh, no. A nervous fist gripped Fred's stomach. Playing with Louis in the den or with the All Stars in the empty Vanguard was one thing—but just the *idea* of playing in front of an audience terrified him beyond belief.

"I don't know if I'm ready for that, Louis," he said. "I think I'll just come along for the ride. Doesn't the plane ticket cost more if I bring my horn?"

Louis shoved a gentle elbow into the boy's side. "No pressure, Pops. You climb up on that stage when you're good and ready—and not a moment sooner."

Whew. . . .

A blue convertible filled with teenage boys and girls pulled up to the curb. "Hey, Pops! What's up, man?"

Hitching up his baggy trousers, Louis strolled over to the car. "Not too much, cats. What are *you* up to? Only good, I hope."

"Oh, just cruisin' around—you know," said the driver, a young man Fred had seen around the neighborhood.

"How's your mama?" Louis asked.

"That doctor you recommended fixed her right up," said the young man. "Thanks for your help."

Louis slapped palms with everyone in the car. "Hey, that's what we're here for, man—helping each other get along. Now you cats be safe tonight. No racing."

"Alright, Pops. Bye!" The car sped off.

Louis sat back on the bench. "I'm willing to bet my chops they'll be racing tonight. Some folks have to learn the hard way."

Little Fred zipped up his jacket. Up and down the avenue the streetlights were turning on. Fat Pete, too, had turned on his neon. A bus going past spit out a cloud of diesel exhaust.

"That smell always reminds me of my mother," said the boy.

Louis chuckled. "Good Lord! The smell of jasmine or of red beans and rice simmering on the stove remind me of my mother, God rest her. Why does bus exhaust remind you of sweet Lorraine?"

"Because when I was little we always took the bus into Manhattan. We'd walk around the Village, she'd poke into all the book stores, and then we'd always have lunch at Shraffts. She said that since I'd always say *hi* to the people on the bus, one old man began calling me *Little Hi*." *Don't start crying. Not here.*

"*Heh, heh*, you *were* a friendly little dude, with the biggest eyes I've ever seen on a child. Even then you were always picking up my horn and slobbering all over it."

The question escaped before Fred knew it: "Louis, why is Dad seeing Sarah Ann Fagan? They're out for dinner *again* tonight and they're always talking on the phone. Doesn't Mom mean anything to him?"

The old musician wrapped an arm around the boy. *Don't cry.* "I don't mean to be mean, Pops, but I think you know the answer to that silly question. No man ever loved his wife more than your father."

"Then why does he want to see her all the time?" *That was loud. Too loud.*

Letting out a deep breath, Louis said: "You know I love you, Fred. You're like a grandson to me—you *know* that—and your father is like my own son. So can I be honest?" The boy nodded. *Uh oh.* "It's a painful fact that this world is full of change. Old folks leave the world every second while babies come screaming in. Last spring's flowers rot to make room for next spring's flowers. Every *second* things are changing— and not always for the better, either. Cats my age find they can't bound up a flight of stairs the way they once did without their hearts kicking the gong around. The changes just keep on coming, too. They never stop. And if a person has trouble dealing with change, then he's going to have trouble dealing with this world."

Fred was angry. "But I've *dealt* with my mother's death. I don't cry about it anymore. I don't bore my friends by talking about it. I don't bother *anybody* about it."

"But we're not talking about your good mother." *That's true. We're really not.* "You don't need me to tell you what a good man your father is. And you *know* that he has suffered as much as you." The boy nodded. "Don't you think he needs a bit of companionship in his life?"

"But he has me." *Now you sound like a baby.*

"That's true, but as you grow older you'll understand that a man needs some female friendship, too. You know, someone to cuddle, someone who smells nice. Nothing personal, Pops, but you smell pretty funky after one of your baseball games, *heh, heh.*"

The same blue convertible filled with the same teenagers once again circled the block.

Keep your voice under control. "I know what you're saying. I know Dad needs someone. But I just thought it would be when I was older—like forty-five."

Louis laughed. "You're a fine cat, Little Fred—and I'll challenge the first dude who disagrees to a duel. Two trumpets at twenty paces, *heh, heh!*" He stood up, stretching. "We're catching an early plane tomorrow for Chicago and Miss Lucille wants my old bones in bed early, so let's ramble."

Little Fred breathed in deeply. The evening sky had become the night sky; an autumn chill was in the air. *Mom's favorite season.* From several stoops floated the voices of folks talking, relaxed. Somewhere a Yankees game was on the radio. The blue convertible once again drove by. "Love ya, Satchmo!" called one of the teens.

"Love you, too, Pops!" growled Louis. "Be safe to-night."

Sixteen

Two fingers grabbed his big toe. "Time to wake up, son."

Little Fred opened his eyes. The window shades were outlined in early morning sunshine.

"My day to make breakfast," said Big Fred. "How does bacon and scrambled eggs sound? It's a cold morning for October."

His son yawned. "Sure. Down in a minute." *Band practice today. That big math test, too. Have to do well or you won't be going to Nashville.* A math whiz named Hannah had been tutoring him for the past week and he felt confident.

Big Fred winced as he watched his son drown his eggs in ketchup. "If I live to be one hundred I'll never understand ketchup on eggs. It's like Billie Holiday with strings: Why mess with perfection?" Aiming a gentle jab at Fred's shoulder, he asked: "Do you think you'll have much homework tonight?"

"Probably. Why?"

"How about you and I grabbing a bite out tonight? I've been in an Italian mood lately. How does *Il Maestro* sound?"

"Sure. Sounds good." *He's feeling guilty for being out so much with Sarah Ann.* "Where's the singer?" *Ouch. That sounded cold.*

"*Sarah* is out of town for a few weeks." Big Fred sipped his coffee. "Big math test today—right?"

"Yup."

"Feel ready?"

"Yup. My friend Hannah explains things more clearly than our math teacher."

"Is she the cute girl with the huge eyes?"

"Yup."

Big Fred smiled. "*Ah!* Beauty and brains in one package—just like your mother."

The boy reached for a second helping of bacon. "Did you know Mom when you were my age?"

"No, I met your mother after I was discharged from the Army. I couldn't understand what a college-educated, smart-as-a-whip, gorgeous woman like Lorraine could see in me. 'Well, it certainly isn't your looks,' she told me once (facetiously, I hope), 'but your ability to *listen*. When I'm talking, I can tell that you're really listening. That's rare in a man.'" Big Fred chuckled. "Lord knows with your mother a man had to be ready to do a *heap* of listening!"

The doorbell rang. Steve and Mark stood on the doorstep, stamping their feet. "Man, it's a crime to be this cold in October!" said Mark. "Hey, Mr. Bradley."

"Hi, Mr. B.," said Steve.

"Morning, gentlemen," said Big Fred. "I'll be home around sixish, son. Then we'll eat *Il Maestro* out of food. Good luck on that test."

"Thanks, Dad."

Steam pouring from their mouths and noses, the boys trudged to school. Old Mrs. Fontaine, wrapped in a bathrobe, was already hunting for one of her cats.

"Good morning, boys," she said. "You haven't seen my Snowball, have you?"

"No, ma'am," said Steve, "but we'll keep our eyes peeled."

"Thank you, boys." Her slippers slipping, Mrs. Fontaine hunted on.

Mark snickered. "I hope Snowball isn't on the cafeteria menu today."

"You never know."

They walked on.

"Did you study for that math test?" asked Steve.

"For two hours. I even missed *Bonanza*," said Mark. "But that doesn't mean I'm going to pass the thing. Now of course Trumpetboy here has his own private big-eyed tutor." He cleared his throat. "Hannah Morrill—the tutor of *loooooooove!*"

Fred couldn't help but grin. "You're a horse's butt—have I ever told you that?"

"Yeah, every other day—and speaking of horses' butts, there's Tim. Hey, Tim!" Mark called out to a chubby bespectacled boy. "Timothy, old boy! Are you *it* today?"

Twice a day—in the minutes before the first period bell and during after-lunch recess—the boys played tag in the tarred schoolyard. *Home* did not exist and the running did not stop. On most days Tim was *it*. He was simply too slow to tag the other boys.

"Yeah, I'm *it*," said Tim, "just for a change."

"You have less than a year to train for the Olympics, son."

"Mark, do you practice at being a fool," asked Tim, "or does it just come naturally?" The boys howled. Despite his owlish looks, Tim could dish it out. Yet as soon as the tag game began, Fred felt badly for him. Huffing and puffing, Tim ran slowly and clumsily, easily outmaneuvered by the others. *Here's today's good deed,* Fred thought, intentionally allowing himself to be tagged. Tim smiled with relief. "Thanks," he whispered.

"No problem."

Bells bellowed across the playground. It was eight

o'clock and the first period of the day was Mr. Kendall's English class. Hannah smiled at Fred as they filed into class. "Ready for the test?" she asked.

"Thanks to you," said Fred. "You should become a teacher, Hannah."

From the back of the classroom came wet kissing sounds—Mark's handiwork.

"Markus," said Mr. Kendall, "since your mouth is so well lubricated this morning, you can read the poem that I'm passing out."

"Glad to, Mr. K." The poem was Langston Hughes' *I, Too, Sing America* and Mark read it with style. For a moment Fred was tempted to show off and tell the class that he had met the poet, but he decided to keep quiet.

"Does this poem remind anyone of anything?" asked Mr. Kendall.

Steve's hand shot up. "That poem we read last week by that bearded guy?"

"Good, Steve. That poem, *I Hear America Singing*, was by Walt Whitman, a poet who lived in the nineteenth century. Now what differe—"

"Hey, Mr. K.," said Mark, "Fred met Langston Hughes last summer."

Every face turned to stare at Fred.

"Is this true, Fred?"

"Yes, sir."

"Why didn't you tell us right away?"

"I don't know. I guess I just don't like showing off like some people I know."

So Fred told the class the story of meeting the great poet. Out of the corner of his eye he could see Hannah watching him. "And I didn't know this but it turned out that Mr. Hughes knew my mother."

Mr. Kendall nodded. "Many people in our community knew her, Fred. She was an exceptional woman."

Be cool. "Thanks, sir."

The next class was history, in which Miss Aylmer discussed riverboat travel on the Mississippi River before the Civil War. Although he nodded sagely every few minutes, Fred let his mind drift away, recalling what Louis had told him about his experiences on the great river. . . .

. . . I'll never forget playing with Fate Marable's band on the S.S. Sidney during the summers of 1919 and 1920. Oh, Lord, those were beautiful days! We'd float into a town and all the folks would crowd on board around dusk. At first some of the white folks would shoot us the old evil eye. Y'see, many had never seen a black musician before. But by midnight they'd be dancing and singing and tossing us tips. Now you see what that good old music can do to folks?

And then during the day I'd sleep late—your grand-daddy would sleep even later, heh, heh—and in the hot afternoons Mr. Marable would help me improve my sight reading skills—just like I'm helping you, Pops. Then I'd sit on the side of the riverboat, my feet dangling out over the water, and watch the tiny towns and the levees and the forests drift past. I'd always have my horn handy and I'd try to play what I'd be feeling, straight and true, with no filter getting in the way.

I'll never forget one steamy afternoon an old white man wearing a funky Abe Lincoln hat was fishing off a pier and he waved at me and I waved back. Then I began to play my horn for him—real slow and easy, like river water—and he stood up and doffed his hat. I wonder how much longer that gentleman lived. . . .

Oh, and once—I think it was the summer of 1920— we tied up for an entire week in the town of Daven-port, Iowa and this young cat named Bix Beiderbecke would bound on board to listen to us. He'd bring his horn and many times he'd step up onstage and play a number or two. What a sound! So clean and precise, yet full of soul. . . .

As Fred daydreamed, his history class sped by.

There was a substitute teacher in science—a skinny man with a bobbing Adam's apple. Mark used the opportunity to goof off but Fred felt sorry for the man and quietly studied his math.

At lunch the friends sat at a corner table.

"Did you guys hear about Upham?" asked Tim.

"No—what?"

"You know how his old man is a detective, right? Well, he brought his dad's handcuffs into Mr. Roy's class this morning—and Roy was dumb enough to ask to be *handcuffed* to the leg of his desk. And it was only after Upham had cuffed him that he realized he hadn't brought the key! Upham's old man was away from the station and it took him over an *hour* to get the message to come to school to unlock old Roy!"

The boys laughed. "What a stooge!" said Mark.

"Remember last year when Roy said I was stupid?" said Steve. "Man, at least I'm not dumb enough to trust Upham."

"He calls everyone stupid," said Fred. "Last year he called me a *troglodyte*. I had to look up what it means: *cave-dwelling beast!*"

Mark snickered. "I wonder if there's a word that means *sad fool who allows himself to be handcuffed by Upham?*"

"Yeah," said Tim, "you find it in the *Rs: Roy*. His picture is even there. He's wearing that nasty green sports jacket."

After lunch came Mr. Perfito's math test and due to Hannah's help, it was a breeze. "How'd you do?" she asked as they filed out of class.

"I think I aced it," said Fred. "I really owe you, Hannah. If I make the honor roll this term I get to go to Nashville in November with Louis Armstrong and his band."

Hannah smiled shyly. "Anytime you need help, Fred, just let me know."

After grabbing his trumpet from his locker, Fred rushed to the band room. Twice a week he finished his school day by playing music. Since Mr. Plamondon had not yet arrived, the band room was buzzing.

"Hey, Fred," said Mike, a freckle-faced trumpeter. "How you doing?"

"Great. I think I just aced my math test."

"Good man! Hey, have you seen Louis lately?"

"No, he's been on the road since last month. He sends me postcards, though."

Mike blew a few notes on his horn. "Do you think you could introduce me sometime?"

Fred adjusted his mouthpiece. "Sure thing. I'll let you know when he's home."

"Thanks." Mike placed a forest of sheet music on his stand. "What are we starting with today?"

"That Sousa medley," said Fred.

"Have you practiced it?"

Fred blew a few practice notes of his own—*loosening up the chops*, Louis called it. "Of course. Haven't you?"

Mike reddened. "Not really. Do me a favor, will you? If I fall apart, try to spot me. I don't think Plamondon likes me that much."

"Sure." *How can you be a musician and not practice? Along with reading, it's the only part of my homework I enjoy.*

When Mr. Plamondon—a large, perspiring man in a tweed jacket—arrived, the band room quickly quieted down. "Good afternoon, ladies and gents," he said. "As promised, we're starting with the John Philip Sousa medley."

For the next half hour the band practiced the medley again and again. *I could play this music in my sleep,* thought Fred. The rhythm was nineteenth century *oom-pa-pa* with no room for improvisation, yet Fred enjoyed blending in his sound with the other musicians'.

"Not bad, folks," said Mr. Plamondon. "Now I have a piece here I'd like us to try—cold." As Fred took the sheet music, he saw that it was Benny Carter's arrangement of *Honeysuckle Rose*. "I've been hearing word of Fred Bradley's skill as a jazz musician," said the teacher, "and I'd like to hear it for myself." *Oh, man, no . . . please leave me alone.* "Now we're going to play to the bottom of the first page and then let Mr. Bradley take it from there."

"I'm not that good," said Fred.

"We shall see," said Mr. Plamondon. "Watch for my signal, Fred. I'll be comping behind you. Play as long as you wish—or can."

"But I've never played this song before." *Who told him I play jazz?*

"Now, class," said the teacher, ignoring Fred. "The essence of jazz is *improvising:* creating music on the spot. I'm able to play many instruments—some of them quite well. I can sight read 'til the cows come home—yet I cannot improvise. I've tried to, many times, but to my chagrin I always run out of ideas. The beauty of a true jazz musician is that he or she *doesn't* run out of ideas. They flow like water. Don't be afraid, Mr. Bradley. You're among friends. One, two, three. . . ."

I can't do this. In a moment the band lunged into the song. *I can't do this!* Soon the teacher's hand shot up. Fred was on his own.

Play what you're feeling that day, Louis had said.

Here goes. . . . Standing, Fred took a deep breath and placed the horn to his lips. Closing his eyes, he played breakfast with his father. He played giving Tim a break in tag. He played acing his math test. He played Hannah's lovely smile. He played going to Nashville with Louis. He played mean Mr. Roy's handcuff dilemma. He played his pride in his mother. He played the honor of being asked to play.

You're doing it!

His mind emptied, Fred sat down as the band brought the song home. From his piano bench, Mr.

Plamondon was the first to clap. His bandmates joined in. *You did it!* The teacher raised his voice above the applause. "That was very nice, Mr. Bradley—very nice indeed."

All in all, it was a fine day in school.

Seventeen

Il Maestro was a darkly lit Italian restaurant in Brooklyn.

"They applauded you?" asked Big Fred. Smiling, Little Fred nodded. "That's incredible, son. I think I was applauded once in school—the day I tripped and dropped my tray in the cafeteria. What does *real* applause feel like?"

Fred thought for a moment. "It's strange. Part of me was embarrassed but most of me was busting."

Lifting his ice-water high, Big Fred cleared his throat. "A toast to my son—master of math and the idol of dozens!" They both laughed. "What did you play in your solo?"

"It's hard to explain, but I simply played my day. I closed my eyes and thought of the different things that had happened. There's no way I could play that solo again in a million years."

"That's jazz, isn't it? *The sound of surprise*, in the words of Mr. Whitney Balliett. Ah! Here comes dinner."

They had both ordered lasagna and it was delicious. "I used to bring your mother here when we were dating," said Big Fred. "I guess you could say it was our place."

You better not bring Sarah Ann here. "How long did you and Mom date?"

"I met her in September, then proposed the following May. I just *knew* that she was the one. We waited a year until we were married then waited a few more years before having you. Your mom wanted to earn her college degree and begin her teaching career before she had a baby."

The words were out before Fred realized it: "I miss her so much."

Big Fred placed his hand over his son's. "I know, Fred. Of course you do. You know, one of the last things she said to me was how much she was going to miss *us.*"

The boy looked down at his plate. *Don't cry. Not here.*

"We should be proud of ourselves. We've survived the worst—I mean the absolute *worst.* You and I have been strong and we've kept on living. I know we had no other choice, but we should *still* be proud of ourselves. I'm sure your mother is."

Dessert was four cannoli. Big Fred chuckled.

"What?"

"I was just thinking of a date your mother and I had. My God, I haven't thought of that evening in quite a while!"

"Tell me."

Big Fred sipped his coffee. "We ate here on a warm summer night. Do you remember my white Chevy? No, of course you don't. I sold it right before you were born. Anyway, your mother suggested a drive to a small lake she knew of out on Long Island.

" 'Is it far?' I asked.

" 'About an hour's drive away. But no one's ever around and we can go swimming.'

"So I took the bait and drove for an hour and a *half* until she pointed out a dirt road. 'Go down there,' she said. The dirt road cut through some mighty thick woods but then opened up into a dirt parking lot right by the shore of this lake. We were the only ones there. Just before I cut the lights I thought I saw a silver dollar—or maybe a half dollar—on the ground.

"'Wait a minute,' I said, stepping out of the car to nab that money.

"As soon as I was out, your mother scooted behind the wheel, slammed the door shut, and zipped off back down that dirt road—leaving me all alone! Talk about dark! And the only sounds were the bullfrogs and mosquitoes. . . ."

Little Fred's eyes were bugging out of their sockets as he listened. *She was a devil!*

"Now I was just going to be cool and wait for Lorraine to return. (Anyways, I was *hoping* she'd return!) I walked down to the water's edge to skip some stones when I noticed that the ground dropped off sharply right before it reached the water. If you wanted to swim, you'd have to walk down this . . . I don't know . . . *incline.*

"Soon I hear my car and then I see the headlights and here comes your mother barreling along. Now she's trying to show off and be funny so she parks the car *right* by the water's edge, with the front end dangling out over *air*. Batting those big eyes at me, she said, 'Were you *scared* out here all by your lonesome?'

" 'Just move on over,' I said.

"Man, were *those* stupid words! One moment I'm watching her fine behind as she's crawling back over to the passenger seat. Then the next moment I'm watching her not-so-fine foot trip the gear shift— and the car begins to *move!*"

"You're kidding!" said Little Fred.

"Wish I was. The car's moving down the incline, your mother is screaming, and I'm hopping alongside trying to be useful! *Splash!* My Chevy is now *in* the water and suddenly seems to want to float across the lake!"

Little Fred laughed out loud. "What did you do?"

His father swallowed the last of his cannoli before replying: "Since your mother was screaming and the car wasn't, I thought it best to attend to her first. I was in chest-deep water—getting deeper all the time—so I swam around the back of my car to the passenger side. Your mother hopped onto my back (which sent me temporarily under water), but then I surfaced and brought her back to shore.

"By this time my Chevy is a *ways* out there, just floating. The headlights were still on, making the water glow an eerie green. Then—*plop!*—I'm watching my poor car sink to the bottom of the lake."

"Quick question," said Little Fred, laughing. "Was it a dollar or a half dollar?"

"It was a washer. So I'm enjoying the absolute biggest laugh of my *life*. At first your mother was all afraid that I'd be furious at her, but I was on my knees punching the ground I was laughing so hard."

"Did you rescue your car?"

"Not that night. First we had to walk *miles* until we found the nearest house. By this time it's past midnight and I felt guilty waking the poor folks up, but they were a cool old couple who let us call a cab. The next morning I called the police and they sent out a crane to retrieve my Chevy. Needless to say, it didn't start."

Wiping the tears from his eyes, Little Fred asked, "Did it cost a lot to fix the car?"

"About four hundred dollars."

"Did you ever get mad at Mom?"

Big Fred wiped his eyes. "Naw. How could a man ever get mad at such a beautiful, beautiful woman?" He looked straight at his son. "I know I've been spending some time lately with Sarah, but don't ever *ever* think that I'm forgetting your mother. She's the first person I think of when I wake up and the last person I pray for before I fall asleep."

"Me, too."

"You're the second."

The two were quiet for quite a while.

"Much homework tonight?"

"Yup. In every subject."

"Then how about you and me getting on home?" Big Fred stood up, stretched. "Another fine meal at *Il Maestro*. How much money do you have on you?"

Little Fred checked his pockets. "Fifty two cents."

"Cheapskate." His father winked. "I guess once again it's my treat." He reached into his pocket. "But when you're a famous jazz trumpeter, you can buy your old man a meal. Deal?"

Little Fred grinned. "Deal."

Eighteen

On a quiet October Saturday afternoon, Little Fred stood by his bedroom window, quietly playing his trumpet. Downstairs the phone was ringing.

"Hello?" he asked, out of breath.

"Little Fred," growled a familiar voice. "That you?"

"Hey, Louis! It's me. Where are you?"

"*Heh, heh, heh*, I'm standing here in the San Diego airport watching Miss Lucille decorate her *chin* with lipstick! We're catching a plane in a few for Honolulu and I thought I'd just give my old friends a ring. Is your dad home?"

"No, he went to work today to earn some overtime. He won't be home until tonight. How's the tour going?"

"Just nifty, Pops. Everywhere we go the folks are digging that good old music. Are you hitting those books? I'm counting on you being with us in Nashville, y'know."

Little Fred smiled. "I'm earning all *A*s, Louis. Last week I aced a big math test. Unless I fall apart, I'm going with you."

"Good man. How's your horn coming along?"

"I'm playing every day. My band teacher had me play a solo last week and I did fine. I wasn't even that nervous. I thought of what you said: 'Just play what you're feeling' and I did great. The kids even applauded me."

"Well, alright, Pops! That's advice that's worked for me for about fifty years now. And doesn't that applause feel mighty fine?"

"Yeah, I could get used to it. Dad and I—"

"Hey, Fred—sorry, man, but they're calling out our flight. Gotta run! Lucille is here wearing a big mess of lipstick sending you her love. Bye!"

Click.

Pouring himself a glass of orange juice, Fred turned on the television and plopped down on the couch. Game four of the World Series was on. Since the Yankees were not in it, he wasn't that interested, *but it's still baseball.* He had just become comfortable when the doorbell rang. *Maybe it's Mark or Steve*, he thought. He was surprised, however, to see Sarah Ann Fagan standing on the front stoop. In a light blue dress, she looked even lovelier than on her album covers.

He opened the door. "Hi, Miss Fagan. My dad's not home."

Sarah smiled shyly. "I know—and please call me *Sarah*. He asked me to come over and wait. He's cooking dinner for all three of us tonight. Do you mind if I come in?"

Dinner? Here? Tonight? Did Dad tell me that? He must have. I wasn't listening again. "It's a free country." *Man, that sounded so dumb. And mean.* "Come in."

Finding a chair in the living room, Sarah said, "Are the Dodgers still winning? They were when I left my apartment."

Little Fred was surprised. "You like baseball?"

"Of course, since I was a little girl. Reminds me of my dad. He was a Dodgers fan and Jackie Robinson was his man. He took me to my first game at Ebbets Field when I was three. In a way I'm glad he didn't live to see his team move to California. It would've broken his heart."

"When did he die?" *Ouch. That sounded brutal.*

Sarah's eyes remained on the game. "Eight years ago last month. I miss him more all the time."

"I know what you mean," said Little Fred. Remembering his manners, he asked, "Can I get you anything? We have ginger ale and orange juice in the fridge. Or you can have water."

"Ginger ale sounds great. Thanks."

In the kitchen Fred also poured some potato chips into a bowl. *She knows how it feels, too. And, man, she's so pretty.* . . .

They sat quietly and watched the game, a Dodger victory. "You know, I should be happy but it just doesn't seem like the same team," said Sarah, standing and stretching. "Well, are you ready for your lesson?"

"What?"

"Didn't Pops tell you? He called me last week from the road and asked if I'd teach you about obliggatos."

"What are those?"

"It's when a trumpeter or saxophonist plays accompaniment to a singer. Louis is a master of it. Mark Wainwright *thinks* he is, but he still has a ways to go. Your dad told me that he has some Bessie Smith records. Do you mind if I play you one?"

Opening up the stereo, Fred pulled out his father's four Bessie Smith albums. Sarah quickly chose the one she wanted.

"Now sit down, close your eyes, and *listen* to this song," she said, lifting the stereo's needle. "The first talent of any musician, I feel, is the ability to truly listen. This is the *St. Louis Blues* and it was recorded back in 1925. Pay close attention to the trumpet player's little fills—*those* are the obliggatos."

The needle landed on the vinyl and in a moment the room was filled with the voice of the "Empress of the Blues," who had died in a car accident in 1937. Her voice—rough, commanding, filled with pain and pride—seemed to say that despite the suffering life had thrown her way, she wasn't going to give in. Then came the sound of a trumpet—muted yet powerful—weaving delicate webs of music in between Bessie's lines. The notes sounded bright, as darting as shooting stars. *It sounds so simple. But Mickey Mantle makes hitting home runs look simple, too.*

"That's beautiful playing," said Little Fred when the song had ended.

"That's our Louis when he was a young man," said Sarah. "Now where's your trumpet?"

In a moment Fred was back downstairs with his new horn. Sarah stood up. "Do you know *Just A-Sittin' and A-Rockin'*?" she asked.

"The Duke Ellington song? Sure."

"Let's play it in D. After every line I'll leave you room to play an obliggato. Just close your eyes and play what you feel."

Here goes. "Can you give me a D?" asked Sarah. Little Fred obliged and in a moment the same voice he had heard in the Vanguard was singing in his living room. *She's as bluesy as Billie Holiday but has that gorgeous Ella tone. Yet there's something totally unique in there, too.* Suddenly he noticed that Sarah had stopped singing and was staring at him.

"What?"

"Did you forget your cue? I'm not playing a solo concert here."

Embarrassed, Fred smiled. "I'm sorry. Start again."

Closing her eyes, Sarah took a deep breath and began again. This time Fred answered each line with his own—trying to capture with his horn the dips and swirls and sly asides Sarah was pouring into the tune. *This is like a conversation*, he thought to himself. *I'm not worrying or even thinking too hard. I'm simply reacting to her notes. I can do this!* At the point when the song should have ended, Sarah dug in deeply and began yet another chorus. *Every one of my lines has been different! I haven't repeated myself once. How long can I keep creating fresh ideas? Wait a minute. Someone's looking at me.* In the doorway stood his father, his mouth agape. Little Fred fell back to earth.

"Why did you stop?" asked Sarah before she, too, saw Big Fred. "Well, aren't you the quiet creeper."

"That sounded great," said Big Fred. "You two were in another world there, weren't you?"

"That was so much fun," said Little Fred. "I just kind of let go."

Sarah wrapped an arm around the boy. "You have a real talent, Fred. There are nights when I'm playing with Wainwright when I just *know* he's thinking about some card game (or girl) after the gig. But *you*!

Your ideas were so fresh. I could tell you were responding to each of my lines."

"Dad hasn't taught me how to play poker yet."

Sarah kissed him on the cheek. "Mark Wainwright better watch his back. I might have a new trumpet player in my band pretty soon!"

Nineteen

Little Fred's nose was flat up against the cold glass. Below sprawled the island of Manhattan, its citizens and visitors busy living out the day of November 21, 1959.

"I remember my first time in an airplane," said Louis. "I was *convinced* that I'd be able to see all the angels in the clouds, playing harps and singing those good old hymns. Too bad I was wrong."

Soon Louis was napping. Reaching for *David Copperfield*, the latest book recommended by Mr. Kendall, Little Fred dove in and was soon on a grassy cliff in Dover, England, watching Aunt Betsey chase donkeys off her lawn.

From behind came the voice of Barney, the band's bald clarinetist. "You *do* like them books, don't you," he said.

"Hey, Barn, I'm the son of a professor."

Barney chuckled. "You remind me of another kid I knew years ago when I was with Duke Ellington's band. His name was Danny. One night in Georgia he hitched a ride on our train and Duke just kind've adopted him. He's still with Duke, too, but now he's (naturally) a grown man."

"Does he play an instrument?" asked Fred.

"A little trumpet, but he's not good enough to play with Duke. Few are. No, Dan does all the copying of music for Duke and Billy Strayhorn. With the way those two write, it certainly keeps him hopping. I just mentioned him because when Dan was a kid *his* nose was always in a book, too."

Diving back into the novel, Fred was surprised when the pilot announced, "We'll soon be landing in Nashville, Tennessee, folks." With a wide grin on his face, Louis woke up. "What do you know," he said, his eyes a million miles away. "In my dreams I was back at the Lincoln Gardens Café, playing with my dear friend Joe Oliver. What do you know. . . ." Stretching and yawning, Louis stood to retrieve his and Fred's trumpets from the overhead rack. "Now remember what your dad and I told you," he said in a low voice. "It's going to be a bit of a shocker."

Ten minutes later, in the airport's echoing lobby, Fred saw what his father and Louis had tried to prepare him for: WHITES ONLY/COLORED ONLY signs posted in front of the restrooms and water fountains. He'd seen photographs—but to stand feet away from these signs, stark white with black lettering, made him feel like, *Sometimes this world is wrong, just plain wrong.*

"Ignore, Brother Fred, simply ignore," growled Louis. "Head held up high—always up *high*. Dignity and honor above all else—that's my motto, Pops. Ahoy! I see Brother Barney's bald dome a-gleaming. A beacon in the night to guide us, *heh*, *heh!*"

Barney, Arvell, Billy, Trummy, and Barrett were at the baggage carousel, waiting for their luggage to appear. Arvell, though, was already holding a bag larger than Fred. "Be thankful you took up the trumpet, you two," he grunted. "Lugging around this old bass sure ain't easy."

Louis grinned. "That's why I pay you rascals such abundant bread."

Outside the musicians piled into three cabs driven by three black drivers. Fred rode with Louis and Barney. The driver was ecstatic. "Louis Armstrong! Barney Bigard! As I live and breathe, the wife's not going to *believe* me!" He glanced in the rear-view mirror. "Hey, Barney, I saw you with Duke in Sweden back in '39."

"You're kidding!" said Barney. "What were you doing there?"

"When my father passed he left me some money. I had nothing doing at the time so I spent a few months bumming around Europe—London, Paris, Stockholm, Rome, Venice. I saw 'em all, right before the war, too. Stayed out of Germany, naturally. Didn't want nothing to do with those Nazis. Saw enough of them in Tennessee."

Barney closed his eyes. "Let's see: It was April, '39 and you wouldn't believe the crowd in the train station in Stockholm when we pulled in."

"Oh, yes, I would," said the driver, "because I was *there*—*and* at the show that night. I swear, the walls of the hall were *quaking*, man! I've never experienced anything like that."

"That was a wild night," said Barney, "and we were so glad to see Sweden, because our train had been stranded all day in Hamburg, Germany. I was sitting next to Rex Stewart and I recall looking out the train window and seeing the Nazis staring in at us. We saw an elderly Jewish couple being kicked around like *dogs* by the Nazis. Man, I was one happy bald man when that train began chugging out of that station. To tell you the truth, I didn't breathe easy until we were out of Germany."

The cab had pulled up in front of a three-story house on a quiet, leafy street.

"What's the name, brother?" asked Louis.

"Henry."

"Are you doing anything tonight?"

"Just listening to the radio and reading the *Defender*."

Louis reached into his shirt pocket. "Not tonight you are—at least not until later. Here're two tickets to our show. Bring your fine lady with our compliments." He also handed Henry a twenty dollar bill. "Keep the change, Pops!"

Soon Louis, Fred, and the five All Stars were being welcomed into the boarding house by a plump, lovely lady named Millie. *She smells like apple sauce*, thought Fred.

"I just made up the beds," she said, "and there's plenty of hot water flowing this morning, so take some hot baths and relax. Are you gentlemen hungry?"

"Does the pope wear a funny hat?" asked Louis and within an hour the musicians—bathed and in fresh clothes—were seated around Millie's table feasting on red beans and rice.

"So Millie, m'love," said Louis, his mouth full, "what's been going on in old Nashville since our last visit?"

Flushed and out of breath, Millie sat down beside Arvell. Opening a napkin, she fanned her face. "Don't you read the papers? Students from the American

Baptist Theological Seminary have been staging sit-in demonstrations at lunch counters *all over* town. Oh, at Woolworth's, Kress', W. T. Grant's, Walgreens. You name the store, they've been there. Lord, I forgot—at McClellan's, too."

"What are the demonstrations about?" asked Fred.

"They want to be able to eat at the lunch counters in those stores, son," said Millie. "The owners allow our folks to shop and spend our hard-earned money in these stores, but we're not allowed to eat at their lunch counters. So these young people have been forcing the issue by planting themselves on the stools until they're arrested. Some folks say they're crazy, other folks say it's beginning to help. Me, I don't know, but I sure admire our young people's courage. Some misguided white folks have been slapping our children around, calling them every unholy name you can imagine, but they simply sit there and don't bat an eye—until they're arrested."

That's stupid! "You mean they don't fight back?"

Millie smiled. "No, son. Most of them are studying to preach the Lord's word and they believe in turning the other cheek. *Nonviolent resistance*, they call it."

"It's a wise choice," said Louis, spooning himself another heap of red beans and rice. "Look who owns the guns and the jails. Fighting with nonviolence is not only fine philosophy—it's fine common sense."

Billy, the band's pianist, chuckled. "Are you going to jaw to a reporter about this, too, Pops?" He looked at the rest of the table. "Remember that Little Rock stink?"

"What happened?" asked Fred.

"Oh, about two years ago," said Barney, "nine of our young people were the first to integrate a white high school in Little Rock, Arkansas. What was the name of that school, Pops?"

Louis' mouth was full. "Central High," he mumbled.

"That's right," said Barney. "You see, Fred, the Supreme Court said way back in '54 that keeping black children out of public schools was now unconstitutional. These nine children were now allowed by *law* to attend this school. But the governor—Faubus was his name—ordered his National Guard troops to keep the kids out. It was disgraceful. Here were our children face-to-face with militiamen with bayonets blocking their way." Barney shook his bald head. "Anyway, a reporter asked Pops his reaction. Now where were we?"

"Grand Fork, North Dakota," said Arvell.

"Yeah, that's right," said Barney, "and Brother Armstrong here let loose with both barrels. What did you call the governor, Pops?"

Louis swallowed before answering. "An 'uneducated

plowboy'—and believe me, that was *too kind* for that sad turkey."

The table broke into a roar. Trummy, the band's trombonist, poked the air with his fork. "And Pops called President Eisenhower 'gutless.'"

Louis' smile stayed put. "Hey, until he sent in the Army he *was*. The man simply needed that fact pointed out to him—which I did. Aw, but I felt bad about hurting old Ike's feelings, so I dashed off a telegram to him: 'If you decide to walk into the schools with the black children, take me along, Daddy. God bless you.'"

"The president sent in the *Army*?" asked Fred.

"That's right," said Millie. "And those soldiers walked the nine students up the stairs of that high school and then accompanied them from class to class from September 'til June."

Louis winked. "See how *enlightened* we are up in Corona, Pops?"

"Has the Army been helping here?" asked the boy.

"No," said Millie. "Our young people are doing it by themselves. For all of us."

"But let's not forget that there are millions of white folks with no hate in their hearts," said Louis. "Anyone who hates—no matter his skin color—just hasn't dug yet what life is all about—and it sure ain't hate. I don't believe the Creator cares about white and black. All *she* cares about is the love in our hearts, *heh, heh*. And that's what I love about our music. The first time I played with Brother Jack Teagarden, we looked at each other and I said: 'I'm a black cat from New Orleans and you're a Texas white boy: *Now let's blow some jazz!*'"

"Amen!" said Minnie, rising from her chair. "Now, I've made some delicious cherry cobbler. Anyone interested?"

They all were.

Twenty

Fred enjoyed helping Barrett set up his drum kit.

"You ever hear Arvell complain about lugging around his bass?" asked the drummer. "Man, that's *nothing* compared with lugging these babies around. You're lucky you took up the trumpet, Freddie. Just place that cymbal right . . . *there*, that's right. Thanks."

Backstage at the Nashville Civic Auditorium the lights were low and conversation even lower. It was only two o'clock in the afternoon and, according to Louis, "at least two hours of rehearsal are ahead, cats, so let's dive in and begin."

Fred was restless; he simply could not sit still. *The whole city of Nashville's out there and I'm stuck in a dark auditorium. I want to explore!* When a song broke down in mid-chorus, he saw his chance: "Um, Louis?"

The old musician mopped his face with a white handkerchief. "Yeah, Pops?"

"Would you mind if I take a walk? I won't go far. Just around the block."

Louis thought for a moment. "Okay. But don't be gone longer than an hour. And stay within shouting distance of this place. Your dad wouldn't appreciate my losing you."

Yeah! Pushing past a set of double doors, he was *outside in actual Tennessee! So this is the South. . . .* Buildings, mostly brick, lined both sides of the street. Back home the November air was already holiday-nippy, but here a bank's thermometer told him it was 76 degrees at 2:11. *I could get used to this weather, man. The only thing snow is good for is cancelling school.* Turning a corner, he walked for several blocks. *This is strange. Why are all these businesses closed up? It's not Sunday.* He stopped. *What's that?* A roar of shouting voices grew quickly louder and closer. The voices sounded angry. *Stop walking and turn back. You're only a few blocks from the auditorium.*

His feet kept moving ahead.

Turn back! Why are you still walking?

Rounding a corner, Fred suddenly found himself face-to-face with a moving mob. *What is this?* Red, furious faces . . . shouting, spitting mouths . . . hard, hateful eyes. . . . All swept past like an undammed river, mere inches from him.

What is this?

Amazingly, no one seemed to notice the boy as he huddled against a brick corner, trying to become invisible. When for a moment the river parted, Fred suddenly saw the cause of this near-riot: dozens of young black men—neatly dressed in jackets, white shirts and ties—marching quietly across the street.

"Not in my lifetime, nigger!" yelled a raw voice.

"*Here's one!*" shrieked another. *He means me!* Grabbed by his collar, Fred was lifted off his feet and hurled into the middle of the street. *Car! Truck! Dead!* his mind screamed. But the street, save for several police officers on horseback, was empty.

"Over here!" called a voice. Scrambling to his feet, Fred dashed into the midst of the marching black men.

"Your knee's bleeding," said a short, muscular young man. "Are you alright?"

Nothing feels broken. I'm walking, aren't I? "Yeah, I'm okay. Thanks."

"I'm John," said the young man. "We're almost there. Just keep walking."

"Almost where?"

John laughed. "What are you, new in town?"

"Yeah, I am," said Fred. "I'm from New York." Remembering his manners, he stuck out his hand. "I'm Fred Bradley."

"Well, Fred Bradley, you've been thrown into a

sit-in demonstration. My group is going to Kress's. You're welcome to join us if you remember one rule: No violence."

Looking across the street at the jeering, hooting mob, Fred asked: "Do they know the rule?"

John laughed again. "No, I mean us. We meet their taunts and sometimes their violence with passive resistance. We don't fight back—at least with our fists. A.J. Muste would say that we fight with *soul force*. But it's only fair to warn you that this might become dangerous."

A.J. Muste. . . . Didn't Mr. Hughes mention him, too? Not wishing to leave the protective shield of black faces, Fred kept quiet and kept marching. Looking about, he was struck by the lack of hatred or fear on the marchers' faces. They looked determined, some even jubilant, yet on no face did he see the grim mask of hatred.

Maybe I can sneak away when they reach Kress's, he thought. *How long did Louis say to be gone? I only left the auditorium about ten minutes ago. Right?*

The marchers made a sudden turn to the left. *Kress's* read the sign above the department store's double doors. A gang of white boys—many wearing red jackets emblazoned with the word *Chattanooga*—blocked their path.

"Stay behind me," said John.

"Ya'll gonna be *hurtin'*, niggers!" shouted one boy.

"Go back to Africa!" shouted another.

Eyes straight ahead, the group of black men, including Fred, marched straight through the gang and into the store. The shoppers—mostly older folks, mostly white—eyed the black men with undisguised disgust as they marched quietly through the aisles. *How can so many guys stay so quiet?* Fred looked back: The gang of young toughs had followed, still taunting and swearing. *There's the lunch counter.* At that moment the lights above the grill were switched off. *Uh oh.*

Grabbing Fred's arm, John whispered: "Since you haven't been through training you can't sit at the counter. Just hang back with those who'll be standing. And watch your brisket."

Along with about a dozen other young men, John found a seat at the counter. An elderly white man who had been seated on one of the circular stools left a quarter on the counter and hustled away. Almost all of the black men were carrying books. Calmly, they now opened them and began to read. No waitresses greeted them. Two swinging doors with plastic windows led into the kitchen. Fred could see several waitresses and a man in a chef's hat leaning against the wall, smoking and smirking.

"*Get the niggers!*" screamed a voice.

Like mad dogs, the white boys tore through the standing black men, their target clear: those seated at the counter. Fred saw a young man with flaming acne punch John in the ribcage. A brutal shot, it did not knock John off his stool.

"Niggers go home!" chanted a group of older shoppers. "Niggers go home!" *They look like somebody's grandparents*, thought Fred. *Heck, they* are *somebody's grandparents. . . .*

Again and again the white boys punched, kicked, spat and slapped at the black men seated at the counter. Yet the protesters sat silently, either keeping their eyes on the pages of their books or looking straight ahead at their images in a mirror above the soda fountain.

I feel useless. Should I do something? But what?

The acne-smeared boy leapt over the counter. "Here, catch!" he shouted to his friends as he tossed them plastic squirt bottles of ketchup and mustard. Sitting stoically, all eyes now ahead, the black men were doused in red and yellow goo as the youths danced around them, chanting, "*Get 'em! Get 'em! Get 'em!*" over and over and over.

Infuriated by the lack of a response, the mob suddenly turned its attention to the group of standing black men, including Fred. "Aren't you man enough to fight?" taunted one red-faced boy. Without warning, he punched Fred in the face. *God! That hurt!* Covering his head with his arms, Fred fell to the floor. *"Kill the niggers!"* A body landed on top of him, knocking the air from his lungs. *"Kill 'em!"* Gasping for breath, Fred could feel more bodies piling over him. *"Kill 'em!"* A heavy foot crashed against the side of his head. The pain was stunning. *I can't breathe!*

From far above whistles blew. A burst of air entered Fred's lungs. *I can breathe!* Bodies were being raised. *More air!*

"Man, are you alright?" It was John's voice, full of worry.

Sitting up, Fred gingerly touched his temple. "I can feel someone's shoe on my head," he said.

"Can you walk? We're being arrested."

"We're being arrested?" Fred was helped to his feet. Several policemen were chatting with the gang who had taunted and beaten the black protesters.

"Let's march, nigras," said one policeman. "The wagons are waiting."

On wobbly, seasick legs, Fred walked beside John, who was lathered in ketchup and mustard. Outside the store a crowd had gathered. *"Rot, rot, rot in jail!"* they chanted, applauding as the protesters were herded into the back of several police vans.

Fred sat beside John on a wooden bench. "You're going to have a nasty bruise there," he said. "Do me a favor: Count backwards from ten to one." The boy did so with no trouble. Wrapping an arm around Fred, John smiled: "Welcome to the Movement, my friend. You've just been baptized with a beating."

As the vans rumbled through the streets of Nashville, the arrested black men—many bloodied, many dripping with condiments—began to sing a song in strong, clear voices. The song began softly, but grew in volume and intensity as the van approached the jail:

You know the one thing we did right
Was the day we started to fight!
Keep your eyes on the prize
Oh, Lord!

Before he knew it, Fred had joined in. Smiling, John leaned close to his ear: "But remember, man, we fight with *nonviolence*!"

Twenty-One

Louis must be so mad by now. He'll never bring me any-where again.

After being fingerprinted and booked, Fred spent the next two hours in a bare cell with John and many others. Beyond the bars, a hallway—lined on both sides with protester-filled cells—ended at a red metal door.

"What brings a New York boy down to Nashville?" asked John.

Fred spoke of his friendship with Louis and of his stroll from the auditorium. All talked ceased. "On the level?" asked John. "You know Satchmo?"

"Really. He's my friend." A feeling of terrible help-lessness seized him. "But I told him I'd only be gone an hour. He must be worried sick by now. I wonder if he's called my dad." *Man, I hope not.* He closed his eyes. *What will Dad say? They even took my fin-*

gerprints! Time passed. Slowly. *I've never seen Louis mad. He'll never take me anywhere with him again—not even to Fat Pete's. I blew it.* Exhausted, Fred soon fell asleep—not aware when the red metal door was unlocked and opened. An immediate buzz filled the cells.

"It's *him!*"

"Hey, Brother Satch!"

"Where's your horn, Satchmo?"

"Fred," said John, "your friend is here."

Opening his eyes, Fred looked up. "*Louis!*"

Tears of relief filled the old musician's eyes. "Oh, thank God Almighty!" he bellowed. "You're alright!" A red-faced policeman stood behind Louis. "Officer, please release my friend here. I'll pay the bail."

"It's fifty dollars, boy," sneered the officer.

Whipping out a roll of bills, Louis peeled off a fifty. "Here you go. And I'd also like to bail out every *man* here."

John spoke up. "No, sir, Mr. Armstrong, that won't be necessary. We certainly appreciate your offer—don't get us wrong—but we prefer to stay here. Right, gentlemen?" A chorus of agreement filled the cells. "You see, paying bail seems to imply that we're guilty of a crime—but we've done nothing wrong. Not to climb up on a soapbox, but we've simply practiced our First Amendment right: 'Congress shall make no law abridging the right of the people *peaceably* to assemble, and to petition the government for a redress of grievances.' That's all we've been doing, officer: peacefully demanding our rights as American citizens."

The policeman spat on the ground.

"Charming," said Louis, turning back to John. "Son, I recognize you from the papers. You're John Lewis, aren't you?" The young man nodded. Reaching through the bars, Louis grabbed his hand. "I respect where you young people are coming from. Keep fighting the good fight, but remember to cover your chops. These people would beat Jesus if he were black and protesting."

"That's enough of that," said the officer, reaching for his keys. "Take your kid and scram."

Shaking his head, Louis turned around to look at each imprisoned man. "If you men do get sprung tonight, come on down to the Civic Auditorium. My band and I will be wailing. Just head to the stage door and my good friend Fred here will let you in."

"Mr. Armstrong," said John, "Fred was very brave, but his head got in the way of a shoe. Have a doctor look it over. Take care, Fred."

Fred shook John's hand. "Thanks, John. For everything."

A few minutes later, as he stepped outside, Little

Fred breathed in deeply. Fresh air had never before smelled so sweet.

Louis was quiet during the cab ride back to the auditorium. After paying the driver, he waited until the cab was gone. They now stood on an empty sidewalk; a streetlight suddenly switched on.

"Alright, Fred. Now tell me what happened."

Tears filled Louis' eyes as Fred described the afternoon. Gently, he examined the bruise on the side of the boy's head. "I'm going to call a doctor to come down and look at you—just to be on the safe side."

"But I'm fine. It doesn't hurt."

"I said just to be on the safe side."

"Are you mad at me, Louis?"

The old musician embraced his friend. "Am I mad at the bravest young man in the whole city of Nashville? What kind of foolish question is *that*?" He looked into Fred's eyes. "My friend, I hope you live to be a hundred and ten, and if you *do*, until your dying day you can be *proud* of what you were a part of today. Do you hear me?" Fred nodded. "Alright then! Now let's scoot inside. The boys have all been worried sick about you and they can't play that good old music with their stomachs all tied in knots. Are you hungry?"

"I'm starving."

"Well, there's a heap of red beans and rice back-stage just waiting for you to dig in. I'm going to call that doctor *pronto* then change into my stage gear. I've got a show to play!"

That night, watching from the wings, Little Fred could not tear his eyes from his friend. Never before had he heard Louis play his horn with so much fire, so much passion, so much soul. *He's blazing tonight!* And although John and his fellow protesters never showed, Fred knew that Louis was playing every note for them.

Twenty-Two

His grandfather's ancient trumpet had grown tarnished. With an old Brooklyn Dodgers t-shirt and a bottle of his mother's silver polish, Fred soon had the old horn gleaming. Downstairs he could hear his father and Sarah laughing as they washed the dinner dishes. *She can sing, she can cook, and she's good looking*, he thought. *Get used to it. She might be around for a while.*

His reflection peered out at him from the trumpet's bell. *Just think of all the music that poured out of this horn. What was New Orleans like back then? Louis always says that my grandfather was a fine musician.* "You'd better believe that little cat could play!" He stood by his bedroom window. A golden haze lit up the horizon. Manhattan's millions of lights were being switched on one by one. Taking a breath, he began blowing into the old trumpet, playing the easy part of

Louis' "West End Blues." There was no anger in the music, only a sort of not-unpleasant sadness that he'd been feeling since his return from Nashville.

Big Fred had been quiet. "I'm sorry you had to go through that, son, Thank God you weren't hurt worse," was all he'd said. Although Louis had called in a Nashville doctor to examine him, his father had insisted on taking him to see Dr. Tuttle, the man who had delivered him. "All hail Fred!" the doctor had said. "The boy whose head can withstand a bigot's boot!"

So he now stood by the window, Manhattan's glow filling the evening sky, softly playing the blues.

"That was lovely," said Sarah, standing in the doorway. Big Fred stood behind her.

"Thanks," said Fred, putting down the horn. *How long have they been standing there?*

"I didn't know you still played that old thing," said his father.

"I love that song!" said Sarah.

"No, no, I meant my father's old trumpet. Louis bought him a new one last summer."

"I haven't played Grandpa's horn in a while. It's not as easy to play as the one Louis gave me, but it still makes music."

"No," said Sarah. "*You* make the music. And it was beautiful." She turned to Big Fred. "Should I ask him now?"

"Be my guest."

"Ask me what?"

Sarah smiled like an excited child. "I'm booked to play at the Vanguard a week from Saturday, and Mark Wainwright, the little rat, has another gig in Harlem that night. So . . . I was wondering . . . if *you* wanted to be my trumpet player?"

"Sure." The word was out in a second. *Wait a minute!*

"Are you *sure* you're sure?" asked Sarah. "I don't want to throw you into a situation you're not ready for."

There's an opening. Take it! Now! "No," he said, "I'm ready. Louis tells me all the time that I'm . . . (*Having trouble saying it, aren't you?*) . . . ready to play in front of an audience."

Sarah wrapped her arms around him. *Man, she smells nice!* "You've made my night. Now we'll rehearse with the band a few times before the show, but if you play with one *half* as much feeling as you just did, you'll blow the audience away."

In a moment Sarah's cab was honking outside. She kissed both father and son on the cheek. "Thank you for a lovely evening, gentlemen," she said. "I'll call you tomorrow to let you know about the rehearsals. 'Night!"

"I'll walk you outside," said Big Fred.

You idiot! What have you gotten yourself into? For a second he was tempted to throw his grandfather's trumpet through the window. *Calm down. Now listen. You played really well that day in school. (But you know the kids in the band). And back in October Sarah said that you played beautiful obliggatos. (But she was the only one in the room—your living room).*

For the next two hours Louis' new horn barely left his lips. Knowing Sarah's repertoire, he played the songs again and again. When he finally laid the trumpet down, his heart was slamming.

"Hey, Fred!" his father called from downstairs.

"Yeah?"

"Come down for a second, will you?"

One living room light shone behind an easy chair, his father, and a book.

"What're you reading?"

Big Fred closed the book. "I took it out of the library today: Dr. King's *Stride Toward Freedom*. It's about the Montgomery Bus Boycotts back in '55 and '56. I think you inspired me. All of Dr. King's ideas about nonviolent protest were put into action by you and those other young people last week in Nashville. You were part of history, son."

Fred flopped down on the couch. His lips ached. "All I know is that I was scared out of my mind. Some of those people were out to *hurt* us. John—that guy

I told you about—told me to picture those bigots as babies and to feel pity for them. But I just couldn't do it. I could only see them as they are *today*—plain evil."

"Did you hate them?"

The boy thought for a moment. "No. I don't think so. But I definitely didn't feel love either."

"I'm proud of you, son. It takes strength not to hate. I think Dr. King's path takes more courage and strength than most people realize."

"Maybe. I really didn't have time to think about it. One minute I'm walking along, and the next minute I'm thrown into this nuthouse. It's easy to be brave about something when you don't have time to think about it."

Big Fred grinned. "Gee, you now have two whole weeks to think about playing at the Vanguard with Sarah."

"Yeah." *Oh, God. . . .*

"You can always back out, you know. She'll understand."

"I know. But . . . I have this dream of being a musician. It's what I want more than anything. Sooner or later, I have to prove to myself that I can play in front of an audience—or else kiss my dream goodbye. You can't be a professional musician and play in your bedroom your whole life."

"I don't know," said his father with a grin. "I could

sell tickets down here." He rubbed the top of his son's head. "I know—bad joke. But you *can* go easy on yourself. You're only twelve."

"Thirteen next month. Lester Young was already a pro when he was my age."

"All I'm saying is that no one here is putting pressure on you. If you honestly feel that this is too much—that you're not ready—then simply say the word. No one will look down on you."

"I know." *But I'll look down on myself.* "Goodnight, Dad."

"Goodnight, son. Love you."

"Love you, too."

As Fred climbed the stairs, he saw his father open up *Stride Toward Freedom*.

Read that book when he's done with it, he thought.

Twenty-Three

How did I get myself into this?

Fifth Avenue's traffic lights were green as far as Little Fred could see. Green light flickered on and off the metal of his trumpet as the cab sped downtown.

"Please slow down," Big Fred told the cabbie.

Yeah—slow down so slowly that we never get there.

"Fine with me, Mac." Slowing down, the driver stopped at a yellow light. "The evening is young and the meter is running."

Man, my mouth is so dry I can't even swallow. How did I get myself into this?

"You alright, son?"

"No, I feel like I'm going to throw up."

"Hey! No cookie tossing in my cab!" said the driver.

Ignoring him, Big Fred said, "It's not too late to pull out of this. Sarah will understand."

Take it! He's offering you a way out. Take it! "No, it's

okay." *Idiot!* "Think of how good I'll feel when the show's over." *Yeah, if you're still alive. Can kids suffer heart attacks?*

"I'm proud of you, son. This takes a great deal of courage."

"Thanks." *Big deal. He's your father. He's supposed to say nice things.*

"You haven't told me what Louis said this afternoon."

"Not much."

Louis' phone call had come just as father and son had returned home from food shopping. "I thought you were ignoring old Satch," said Louis over a scratchy connection from Dallas, Texas.

"Dad couldn't find his keys," said Fred. "Thanks for calling, Louis."

"I wish I could be there for you, Pops. You know that. But I'll be home next week for Christmas and you can tell me all about it. Remember: Just close your eyes and play how you're feeling."

"I'll be feeling terrified. Will that make good music?"

And now he was feeling truly terrified as the cab pulled in front of the Vanguard's red awning. As usual, Max was outside, his steamy breath rising to the sky, yabbering with his waiting customers. "The two Freds!" he called, rushing over to shake hands. "Sarah's already here. Go on down."

Each step down into the club felt like Fred's last. He barely made it in time to the toilet to vomit. "Are you alright?" his father called from outside the stall.

Little Fred blew his nose. "Actually, I feel a bit better. Don't tell Sarah."

In the hallway, Sarah, resplendent in a red dress, was grinning. "You're looking a tad pale—quite a feat for a black boy. Now stand back." She looked him up and down. "I'm glad you two let *me* pick out the suit. You're looking fine, Fred. I'll be right back."

Little Fred sat down on a crate of cola bottles. *Why did I say I'd do this? I could've said, "No way!" and she wouldn't have held it against me.* He looked down at his black shoes, polished that afternoon by his father. *Simply run away! Say that you need some air, walk upstairs, then run for the subway. She still has four musicians in her band for God's sake. The world won't end. Playing without a trumpeter won't kill her.* His father patted his shoulder. *No, that's going back on your word. Plus, Dad would be worried. You're committed now. Hey! Maybe you can pretend that you've fainted on stage and they'll call an ambulance and carry you out of this place. No, that would be wrong. Remember the time they carried Mom out of our house and put her in an ambulance? It would be wrong to fake it.*

Smiling, Sarah took Big Fred's hands, and they talked quietly in a corner.

Fred had attended two rather rushed rehearsals. Only one musician in Sarah's band—the white pianist Dave—had shown any interest in him. The others had treated him as a pesky nuisance. "You'll do fine, kid," Dave now said as he grabbed a warm cola from a crate. "How're you feeling? You don't look so hot."

"I feel like I'm going to throw up again."

Half the bottle had vanished in one swig. "Just don't ralph in the piano, that's all I ask. Aim it in the direction of Pete's bass."

"I heard that!" called a voice from the men's room.

"You were supposed to," said Dave. He turned back to Little Fred. "It's too bad you don't wear glasses like me."

"Why?"

"I sit down on the stool, take these babies off, lay them beside me, and I can't see two feet in front of me. The audience doesn't exist. I tell you, being near-sighted is a blessing in this business."

"Fred has twenty-twenty vision," said Big Fred. "It's a blessing in baseball."

"But, unfortunately, not in music," said Dave. He gently punched Fred on the arm. "Just remember: Aim it toward Pete's bass."

"I heard that!" screamed Pete, still in the men's room.

Sighing, Dave wandered off.

Much too soon Max was announcing Sarah's band, who were to play one number, Duke Ellington's *In a Mellow Tone*, before she took the stage. In rehearsal, Fred had played it cleanly and with feeling. "I have to use the bathroom," he said to Sarah. "Do you mind if I sit this one out?"

Sarah studied the boy. "No, that's fine. The number will last about ten minutes." She looked at Big Fred. "*Is he okay?*" she whispered.

No, I'm not. I'm going to fall on my face. "I can hear you. Yes. I'm fine. I just have to use the bathroom, that's all."

Luckily, the tiny bathroom was empty. Little Fred locked himself inside the one stall and vomited again. *I can't do this. What made me ever think I could be a musician? The only reason Louis and Sarah encourage me is because I'm a kid. I should've stayed in my bedroom. That's the only place I'll ever play music.*

"That sounds pretty nasty," said his father from outside the stall.

Fred waited a few moments. "I think I'm done. There's nothing else to throw up." Walking out, he cleaned his face and blew his nose.

"Sarah has more than enough musicians for the show," said Big Fred. "The saxophonist can cover for you all night. What's his name?"

"Joe."

"Not the friendliest guy."

He's a jerk. Always sneering at me like I'm a stupid little kid. Imagine his sneer if I back out now. . . .

"No, I want to do this. I'm fine. Really."

Leaning down, Big Fred whispered to his son, "*I* couldn't do this. You have guts, Fred."

No, I don't. I just don't want to see Joe the Jerk sneering at me. I don't have any guts at all.

Sarah poked her head into the men's room. "Max is just about to announce me. Do you want to go on?"

No! "Where's my horn?"

"Right here," said Sarah. "I'm holding it."

Max's voice boomed from the stage: "And will you please give a warm welcome to a truly rising star: *Miss Sarah Ann Fagan!*"

Big Fred straightened his son's tie. "I couldn't be more proud of you. Remember that."

What did he say?

Sarah handed him his trumpet and he followed her into the glare of the Vanguard's stage lights. Not one space in the club was empty. Clapping warmly, people sat in every seat and stood lining the walls. Following the red speckles of Sarah's dress, Fred felt his feet step up onto the stage. He took his place beside Dave's piano. "Take it easy, kid," said the pianist. "This ain't life or death."

Maybe not to you. "Yeah."

Sarah's voice sounded miles away. "Thank you very much, ladies and gentlemen. I'd like to begin with a beautiful song by Jule Styne and Sammy Cahn: *Time After Time.*" Dave played the opening chords, Joe followed with a smooth tenor chorus, and Sarah, her eyes closed, dove into the song. *You know this song*, Fred thought. *You've practiced playing obliggatos with her. You've played this song alone about a hundred times. Now play!* Raising the trumpet to his lips, he took a breath—then quickly lowered the horn. Joe, rolling his eyes, took another chorus on tenor. Turning, Sarah looked at him. "*Take your time,*" she mouthed, before returning to the microphone.

Maybe I'll sit this one out, too. Just get used to being on stage.

Joe was now playing an improvised solo with not a trace of a sneer in it. Looking out into the audience, Fred saw that no one was looking at him. *Where's Dad?* Every eye was either on Joe or on Sarah, who stood tapping her right foot and smiling at her saxophonist.

I can't sit this one out. Remember rehearsal? I'm supposed to play a long solo next!

Sure enough, as Joe wound down his solo, he took a step back and nodded to Fred, as if to say, "Your turn, kid."

Once again Fred raised the trumpet to his lips. *You can do this!* Once again he took a deep breath. *Every-*

one has faith in you. You can do this! Closing his eyes, Little Fred pressed his lips to the mouthpiece and began to play.

Only a nasty squawk erupted from his horn.

No!

Again, he breathed in deeply.

The nasty squawk had only grown louder.

"Nice," said Joe out loud, sneering for all the world to see.

Tears in his eyes, Little Fred looked over at Sarah. "It's okay," she mouthed. "It's okay. Try again."

This time no sound at all came from his trumpet. Several people in the audience laughed and the song ground to a halt.

Get me out of here!

Dropping his trumpet, Fred leapt off the stage, knocking into a table. Several glasses of wine and beer crashed to the floor. "All over my dress!" screeched a woman. *Get me out of here!* Reaching the bottom of the staircase, he took the stairs two at a time and was soon standing beneath the Vanguard's red awning. His heart was trying to punch a gaping hole through his chest. *It's cold! Who cares? Get away!* As he dashed across Seventh Avenue, a cab slammed on its brakes. "Ya wanna get killed?" screamed the driver.

I don't care! Get away! Get away!

Twelfth Street was quiet, lamps glowing from behind its many windows. His footsteps and his panting breath were the only sounds he could hear. Finally, utterly drained, he collapsed on the stoop of a darkened brownstone. Once again he vomited. *You're a failure.*

A hand on his shoulder. *A cop?* "This will pass, son." Tears filled Big Fred's eyes. In one hand he held his son's coat, in the other his trumpet. "Like everything, this will pass." Like a young child—*like a baby!*—Fred began to cry into his father's shoulder. *You're a failure! You'll never be a musician. You were just kidding yourself. Sucker!*

"*Shh*," said Big Fred, rocking the boy like his mother once had. "That's it. . . . Let it out. . . . It's alright. . . . Let it out. . . ." *I'm a failure. A failure.* "I love you, son." *How can anyone love a failure?* "*Shh*. . . . It'll be alright. I promise. Everything will be alright."

Twenty-Four

Four boys walked home from church. A mid-December thaw had enveloped Queens in balmy air and the good folk of Corona were out and about.

"Do you think I'll fry in Hell for thinking about Reverend Robert's wife?" asked Steve.

Mark kicked a stone off the sidewalk right smack into a drain, where it landed with a *plop!* "Are you thinking about her cooking?"

"No. . . ."

Tim snickered. "I'll bet he's thinking of her oven, though!"

The boys, even Fred, laughed. An old lady holding a child's hand shot them a glance.

"Man, are you *kidding*?" asked Mark. "For lusting after a reverend's wife, God sends you to the deepest darkest *pits* of Hell! You'll be roasting forever, son. Be sure to send us a postcard."

"Hey," said Steve, "if Tim ever goes to Hell it'll take *forever* to cook all that flesh."

"When in doubt," replied Tim, "go for the fat joke. The idiot's escape."

Fred spoke up. "Remember what Mr. Kendall said last week? That we can't control our thoughts, only our actions? So that would mean our Steven is safe. To be honest, I sneak a few peaks in the old gal's direction myself."

"*Awwwwww!*" His three friends tackled Fred onto a lawn beside the sidewalk. Grabbing up the child, the old lady crossed the street. The boys did not notice. "Speaking of fat, anyone have any loot for Fat Pete's?" asked Mark.

"Not me," said Tim. "I put it all in the collection basket. Last time I checked, though, the benches were still free."

So the four friends gathered on their favorite bench across from Fat Pete's to talk and watch the Sunday morning world drift past.

"So what's the mystery, Trumpetboy?" asked Mark. "Why won't you tell us about last night?"

Fred sighed. "You know, I woke up this morning in a good mood. I *knew* that something was bothering me, but for a few seconds I couldn't remember it. I didn't *want* to remember it, but then it all came rushing back anyway."

"What?" asked Tim. "It couldn't be *that* bad."

"Oh, no?" said Fred. "Just listen to this. . . ." And without leaving any detail out, he told his friends about the debacle in the Vanguard.

Mark whistled. "Oh, man. . . ."

Steve shook his head several times. "You knocked the drinks off the table? Right into her *lap?*"

"Yup. She looked like she wanted to kill me."

Tim smiled. "Is that all? You were too nervous to blow your trumpet and you knocked over a few glasses. That's it? From your face in church, I thought you'd killed somebody."

"Is that all?" said Steve. "He ruined the show and ran out of the joint! If I was Fred I'd want to *die!*"

"I've seen hamster droppings with more brains than you, Steve," said Tim. "Think about it: How much do adults *really* care about us? I mean, really. Do you think a bunch of adults are upset today because some kid—whose name they don't even know—couldn't play his horn? You think *that* ruined their day? Man, they've probably forgotten about it already. Except, of course, the lady with the damp lap."

Hmm, I didn't think of it that way.

"Plus," said Mark, "it'll make a great story someday."

"Heck, it's a great story now!" said Tim.

You know, they're right: It is *a great story.*

"Have you told Louis?" asked Mark.

Three girls holding ice cream cones walked out of Fat Pete's. They waved but the boys did not notice.

"No. He called me yesterday to wish me good luck, too. He said he'll be home right before Christmas."

"What are you going to tell him?"

"That I've been fooling myself. That I was never meant to be a musician. I'm going to give him back the trumpet he gave me and tell him to give it to someone else. Someone who can play in front of people without puking and crying."

Steve and Mark shook their heads in sympathy—but Tim punched Fred on the shoulder, almost knocking him off the bench. "You're an idiot! You think you're the first person who's ever made a fool of himself? Ask the old fat boy here. I make a fool of myself every time we play sports."

"But it's different," said Fred. "Sports don't matter to you. Playing the trumpet means everything to me."

"Wrong again, idiot," said Tim. "Sports mean a *lot* to me. I'd give anything to be a good athlete and not always be the last one chosen for every team. Don't you think that hurts?" *Yeah, I see how embarrassed you are. Sorry.* "You have a talent, man. I've heard you play. You're *good*. And if you throw your talent away just because of some stupid night in front of some useless strangers, then you're a true idiot."

"Hey," said Mark, "that's the hundredth time you've called him an *idiot*. Lay off."

Fred stood up. "No, Tim's right. I *am* an idiot." *Did Mom ever give up? She fought until the very end.* He shook Tim's hand. "Thanks. Next time we choose teams, I'm choosing you right off. See you guys later."

"Where're you going?" asked Steve. "We're going to shoot hoops."

"You guys can," said Fred. "I'll catch up with you later."

His three friends watched him dash off. "You know," said Mark, "he *is* an idiot. But you still have to love old Trumpetboy."

Big Fred was in the backyard hanging damp sheets on the clothesline. "How was Reverend Robert's wife looking?" he asked.

"Pretty fine, actually."

"There's a grass stain on your new slacks."

"I know. The guys tackled me."

"Sarah called to see how you were doing. She said the world kept spinning after we left. It would be nice if you called her later."

"I will." Grabbing a handful of clothespins, Fred helped his father. "I want to apologize for last night."

"Apologize? For what?"

"For being such a baby. I'm almost thirteen—I

could've handled myself much better. If I'd just nodded to Joe he probably would've taken another chorus. Running off like that was childish. I'm sorry if I scared you."

Big Fred grinned. "Well, you *did* take a year off my life when that cab almost hit you, but after that I was impressed with your speed. Man, oh, man! It feels like an April day! Go grab our gloves. Let's you and me play some catch."

Soon the baseball was flying back and forth across the backyard.

"You know," said Little Fred, "this morning I was ready to never pick up my trumpet ever again. I was giving it all up."

"Nice catch. You've changed your mind?"

"Yeah. It was something my friend Tim said. He made me realize that I'm not at the center of the universe. Last night I thought I was."

Holding the ball for a moment, Big Fred said, "My father wasn't one to give much advice, but once he said to me: 'The child believes he's the most important person in the world. The adult knows that he's no more important than anyone else.' Then he added, 'I guess I'm still a child.' The man knew himself." He threw the ball. "Isn't it something? His twelve year old grandson is more of a man than he ever was."

For several minutes they quietly played catch.

"Do you know what I want for you, son?"

"A woman who looks like Reverend Robert's wife?"

Big Fred grinned his gap-toothed grin. "Well, that, too—but I want you to have a *career*. Whether it's in music or some other field, I want you to do something you're *proud* of. Now what I have is a *job*. Nothing wrong with it—it pays the bills—but it doesn't really bring me any pride. *You're* the one who does that."

Don't cry two days in a row, Chump. "Thanks."

"So you're not giving up on music?"

"No."

"Good. You see, I'm really a selfish dude. I love having my free nightly concerts while I'm reading the papers."

"Miles Davis wrote a song about you, Dad."

"I know—*Freddie Freeloader!* Ha!"

Father and son played catch until their out-of-shape December arms ached.

Twenty-Five

At dawn on Christmas Eve a light snow began to fall over Corona. By nine o'clock the world was smothered in white. After his father left for work, Little Fred had the house to himself; he practiced his music all morning until the doorbell rang.

"Merry Christmas, Mr. Zimmerman," he said.

"Happy holidays to you, Fred," said the mailman, stamping his feet. "Shoot, it's cold! Here you go—special delivery."

A red envelope covered with familiar handwriting—yet with no stamp or postmark—was placed in his hands. Ripping it open, he read:

Brother Fred!

What are you waiting for, man? Miss Lucille is out having her hairdo worked on and old Pops is home alone just sitting around. Drop on by—and bring your horn!

Ho! Ho! Ho!
Santa Satch

In a whirlwind Fred yanked on his galoshes, flew into his winter coat, crammed a wool cap on his head, and dashed outside. The snow was still falling and the world seemed quiet and muffled. No one was about as he trudged the three blocks to 107th Street, his new horn safe and dry beneath his coat.

"Right on time!" growled Louis, standing in the kitchen doorway. "Armstrong's Famous Cocoa (patent pending) is almost brewed."

Fred hugged his dear friend.

"Good to see you, too, Pops. Been quite a spell, hasn't it? Here, take off those boots. We don't want to get the old evil eye from Miss Lucille for messying up her floor."

Soon the two were seated at the kitchen table, sipping their cocoa and talking. From Louis' upstairs den flowed the sweet strong sound of his horn. "That's from a show in Milan last month. Not too shabby if I do say so myself—and I *do*!"

Fred began to tell Louis about his brief performance in Sarah's band, but the old musician stopped him. "Your daddy told me all about it on the phone. Someone's coming over soon and we'll discuss it with him." *Who? Dad?* "You hungry? Mama Lucy mailed up some mighty fine fruitcake. Mr. Zimmerman just delivered it."

"Sure. Who's Mama Lucy?"

Louis cut the boy a huge slice. "Haven't I mentioned her before? You sure? Well, she's my younger sister—my *only* sister. About a foot taller than old Satch and a mile finer, yessir. Mama Lucy and Miss Lucille don't exactly see eyeball to eyeball, if you catch my meaning, so my sis stays in her cozy crib in New Orleans. Can I brew up more cocoa?"

"Sure, thanks." The snow was sticking to the kitchen windows and there was no place in the world that Fred would have rather been.

"Man, will you look at all that beautiful snow piling up. And Old Satch can simply sit on his plump can for the next month—imagine that!"

"Alright," said Louis an hour later, lying back on the couch in his den. As usual, he was wearing his favorite white socks and tan sandals. "Now I want to hear *St. Louis Blues*. My eyes will be closed but my ears will be *wide open*."

Relaxed and almost confident, Fred brought his horn to his lips, inhaled, and blew chorus after chorus of (in Louis' words) "sweet, pure, *low-down* blues. Man, you were *feeling* that—I could tell."

Fred nodded. "When I'm not nervous, music is so

easy to play. I hear the notes in my head and a second later they're pouring out of my horn."

"I hear you, Pops. Those are the moments I truly love: When I'm not playing that old horn but *myself*. My thoughts shoot right through my fingers and chops into pure music. It doesn't always happen, but when it does—"

"'*Lo!*" shouted a voice from downstairs. "Any ol' moldy figs at home up there?"

"*Heh, heh, heh!* I know *that* rascal's voice. Diz! Up in the den, brother!"

In a moment a smiling Dizzy Gillespie appeared in the doorway, his horn-rimmed glasses fogged up, melting snow dripping off his shoulders and black beret. "Man, don't you just love it when Mother Nature takes over?"

"Only when I have a cozy crib to crawl into," said Louis. "Great to see you, Diz. This here is my dear friend—"

"Let me guess," said Dizzy, his arms crossed, a finger placed on his chin. "Is this the fine Fred—the warrior prince of Nashville?"

"The very same, " said Louis.

Fred shook hands with one of his heroes, the artist whose solos on recordings such as *Groovin' High* and *Dizzy Atmosphere* he could flawlessly recreate. "Great to meet *you*, Mr. Gillespie."

"There are no *misters* among musicians, my man," said Diz. "Now is it your dad who's seeing Sarah Ann?"

"Yeah."

"Lucky dog. A whole mess of cats are jealous of *him*, let me tell you! She's one lovely lady. Can sing, too."

Louis chuckled. "Fred here sat in with her band at the Vanguard a few weeks back."

His coat, beret, and shoes removed, Dizzy plopped down on the couch. "Don't say? How'd it go?"

Thanks a lot, Louis. "Don't ask," said Fred.

Dizzy lowered his horn-rim glasses. "Pretty brutal?"

"You could say that," said Fred. "I couldn't get a sound out of my horn and then I ran out of the club."

"*Whooo-eeee!* Max must've loved that!"

"*Heh, heh, heh.* Our poor boy here was on the verge of throwing in the towel along with his horn, but luckily he's reconsidered. Now how many times have you fallen on your face, Diz?"

"Oh, Lord! Higher than I can count!" Dizzy looked at Fred. *He's as nice a guy as Louis!* "Fred, I've seen musicians fall asleep on the stage and miss their cues and shut down an entire band. I've seen those men fired on stage on the spot. I saw a bandleader get smacked with a spitball once on stage and wind up getting his be-hind nicked with a knife." Louis began to chuckle. "Man, if you're going to be a jazz musician, you have to get *used* to failing, because you're flying by the seat of your pants every night."

"But I couldn't even get *one note* out of my horn," said Fred. "The only sound I made that night was me throwing up."

"Yeah, but at least you sang your song in the can," said Louis. "I've seen musicians so nervous they vomited into five-thousand-dollar pianos! I once saw old Al Capone smack some sick dog's head for doing that."

"Did he shoot him?" asked Dizzy.

"Naw, just frightened him so badly that the poor cat needed new britches."

Cleaning his glasses with his shirttail, Dizzy said, "Fred, the only failures in this world are the folks who don't *try*. You just can't let a little mishap slow you down. You have to keep on trying—even if you have a dozen more mishaps ten times *worse* than that one. Just keep on trying. That's the secret of making it in music—and in this world."

"Amen, Brother Gillespie!" said Louis, leaping up to switch on his reel-to-reel tape player. Immediately the den was filled with the warm, golden sound of his horn.

"Man!" said Diz. "You're sounding mighty tasty,

Pops. When was this recorded?"

"Last month in Milan. Lucille and I spent the entire day strolling through museums, checking out the fine art, and then that night me and boys blew up a storm."

"You're blowing *fiiiiine*, Pops. What are you—sixteen or seventeen years older than me?"

Louis chuckled. "Depends on the day I'm asked."

"Man, I just hope I sound as sweet as this when *I'm* an old grizzly."

"Just take care of your chops, Diz," said Louis, "and you will. Man, all this jawing and philosophizing is making me *hungry*. Let's go downstairs to watch this old grizzly whip up some grilled cheese sandwiches."

Outside a snowplow rattled past. The storm seemed to have gained strength. Louis filled the kitchen sink with soapy water.

"Nothing against the ladies, Diz, but isn't it nice when they go out for the day?"

"Yes, indeed, Pops."

This is great, thought Fred, sitting at the kitchen table. *I'm just going to keep quiet and listen. . . .*

The dishes soon washed, Louis sat down, too. "It's funny. I've had comfortable bread for over thirty years now, but I *still* appreciate a warm room to sit in when it's cold outside."

"I know what you mean," said Dizzy. "My father up and died when I was almost ten and, boy, was it rough after that. My mama took in washing and sewing and was able to squirrel some money away. But then the president of our local bank skedaddled with most of the town's money. Can you imagine? My poor mama lost every *penny* she had managed to save. You would've had to *double* our money to make us poor after that!"

Louis' eyes were fixed on the falling snow. "When did that old horn bite you?"

"Soon after my father died," said Diz. "Santa Claus brought my next door neighbor, a dude named Harrington, a trumpet for Christmas. I saw it hanging on his family's tree and went absolutely crazy! 'Go ahead and try it,' Brother Harrington said. Lucky for me, he didn't get into the horn at all, so I was free to trot on over to use it whenever I wished—which was constantly. How about you, Pops?"

Louis told Dizzy the story of the Karnofskys' junk wagon. "But I didn't *really* start to learn music until I met Professor Peter Davis at the Colored Waifs' Home for Boys."

"But you weren't an orphan," said Fred. "You had your mother and Mama Lucy, didn't you?"

Louis looked sheepish. "I got into a bit of a scrape with the law and a judge sent me to the Home. Best thing he could've done for me. The teachers taught me how to read and write and I met Professor Davis."

"What was the scrape?" asked Diz.

"Alright: It was New Year's Eve 1912, so I was about your age, Fred. You see, I had me a little singing quartet—called ourselves the Singing Fools, *heh, heh*. We'd sing for pennies on street corners. So we headed out that fine evening to earn us some sweet bread singing for the revelers. Maybe a bit of dancing, too.

"Believe it or not, I can *still* recall a song I sang that night." Louis cleared his throat. "Let's see: '*My Brazilian beauty down on the Amazon. . . . That's where my baby's . . . gone, gone, gone. . . .*' Boy, the crowd liked that song! I was collecting those coins as fast as folks could throw 'em. Of course, I was planning on giving most of 'em to Mayann the next morning.

"Now get ready for the sad part of the tale. I was just a stupid kid who'd gone rummaging through a trunk belonging to Mayann's latest boyfriend. And beneath some shirts I found a loaded .38 pistol. So I tucked that baby into my pants—not to shoot anyone, y'understand, but to fire up into the air at midnight.

"So midnight hits and the entire world is going mad. Some little dude across the street whips out a puny cowboy six-shooter and begins firing it up into the sky. Now my homeboys know that I'm carrying, so they start yelling, *You, too, Dipper!* So I whips out my stepfather's .38 and commence firing that baby up to Heaven! It's making a heck of a lot more noise than the six-shooter and I'm feeling like a mighty big man when—*whoops!*—some strong hands grab me by the shoulders. I'd been nabbed by a detective! Even though I cried and cried, he hauled me to juvenile court where I was thrown in a cell for the night. Lord, that bed was hard! The next morning I'm hauled in front of a judge who says—not knowing that he's saving my life: 'I'm sentencing you to the Colored Waifs' Home for Boys.'"

"You must've been so scared," said Fred.

"Never been so scared in my life. Y'see, I didn't have a wonderful father like you do, pointing out to me right from wrong. Seemed that Mayann had a different boyfriend (and I had a different 'stepfather') every month. And *that's* the reason why I fell into mischief. And *that's* how I found the finishing school that gave old Pops his class and polish, *heh, heh!*"

Opening the refrigerator, Dizzy poured himself a glass of orange juice. "And this Peter Davis showed you your way around the horn?"

Louis held out his glass for a refill. "Not right away. At first the good professor didn't like Little Louis at *all*. I guess he figured that since I was from around Liberty and Perdido—a part of New Orleans folks called *The Battlefield*—that I was drop-dead *evil*. He ran the Waifs' Home orchestra, which I wanted to join in the *worst* way, having been blowing my little horn with the Karnofskys, y'see. So I hung around the band's rehearsals, just itching to join in the worst way.

Anyways, one day Professor Davis said to me, 'You're not as bad as I thought. You were simply mixed up with the wrong company.' (Little did he know that the 'wrong company' was not my homeboys, who were straight, but my mama's boyfriends). When he asked me to join the orchestra my entire world opened up. Peter Davis gave me the keys to the kingdom."

He looks like he's going to cry!

"Yup," said Dizzy, "sometimes it just takes one person giving you a bit of his or her time to change your whole life. For me it was Miss Alice Wilson, my third grade teacher. She knew that I was playing old Brother Harrington's borrowed horn, so she arranged to nab me a school horn. Lord, she was a beautiful woman! She led a little school band: trumpet, trombone, snare and bass drums, with herself on piano. The day she asked me to join that band meant more to me than the day Cab Calloway asked me to join his."

"I hope you didn't toss spitballs at *her*, too!" roared Louis.

Dizzy's orange juice went down the wrong pipe.

"That wasn't me!" he spluttered. "I swear to God that wasn't me!"

"What?" asked Fred. "What?"

"Sorry, Pops," gasped Louis, tears of laughter running down his cheeks. "*That* tale's for when you at *least* have some whiskers!"

Twenty-Six

That evening the snow was still falling when father and son returned home from church to an empty house.

Big Fred walked upstairs. Turning on the television, Little Fred watched carolers singing by Rockefeller Center's skating rink. During *Silent Night* the phone rang. Louis' bullfrog voice was surrounded by noise. "Fred! We're having a holiday jam session down at Fat Pete's. Grab your dad and come on down!"

"Who is it?" asked Big Fred from upstairs.

"Louis. He wants us to head to Fat Pete's. Something about a jam session."

"Tell him we'll be there."

"*Ho! Ho! Ho!*" roared Louis.

Sitting on a kitchen chair, Big Fred pulled on his galoshes. *He looks so tired.* "You okay, Dad?"

Sighing, Big Fred wrapped an arm around his son.

"I'm sorry. I don't mean to bring you down on Christmas Eve. I'm just missing your mom even more than usual. Church made me remember all the Christmas Eves when she was sitting with us, singing out of key. She feels very far away tonight."

She feels far away every night. What's so different about tonight?

The snow covering the sidewalks crunched beneath their boots. Hanukkah menorahs and Christmas tree lights shone in front windows, pouring cheerful light into the darkness.

Fat Pete's was packed. A distinguished older gentleman sat ramrod straight before a portable electric piano. Beside him, dressed in full Santa suit (minus the beard), stood Louis, trumpet in hand. "Now here's two of my dearest friends, folks. Happy holidays to Fred Bradley and Fred Bradley!"

The crowd, most of whom were friends, clapped and cheered. Steve, Mark, and Tim, seated with their families, waved from across the room. Big Fred found two seats in a snug corner.

"Now here's a good old good one," said Louis, launching into a swinging version of *Christmas Night in Harlem*. The old gentleman played the piano with gusto, Louis blew for all he was worth, and the people began to clap with the beat. Big Fred nudged his son. "See the old pianist?" he whispered. "He's Ed

Milk, my seventh grade English teacher, one of the very best. My mother and I had just moved up to New York from Tennessee, and Mr. Milk made me feel welcome. That old man is another reason I love reading so much. He'd close the blinds, light several candles, and read Edgar Allen Poe to us. I've never forgotten that."

For the next hour Louis and Mr. Milk transformed Fat Pete's into a rollicking, joyous holiday jazz club. Every voice grew hoarse with singing. At one point, Louis said, "Now, folks, let's not forget that this is also Hanukkah season for our Jewish brothers and sisters. This song was taught to me many moons ago in old New Orleans by a wonderful woman named Mrs. Karnofsky. This one's for her and her fine family, God rest 'em."

All were quiet as Louis played a lonely, foreign-sounding tune—a tune that sounded from another age. The old musician's eyes were closed as he poured love and respect from his heart through his horn. As the last note faded into nothing, the room was silent for several seconds. "That was just lovely," said a woman's voice just before everyone burst into applause.

"Thank you, folks," said Louis. "It's an honor to play my horn for you tonight—especially with Brother Ed Milk on the ivories."

It was close to midnight in the Bradley home. Big Fred, Louis, and Little Fred sat in the living room, sipping cocoa and talking. Still in his Santa suit, Louis reached into a pocket, pulling out a folded envelope. "This is for you, Fred. Your dad and I have been cooking it up for quite a while."

Ripping open the envelope, the boy read the letter inside:

To the Bearer (that's you, Little Fred, heh heh):

This piece of paper entitles the bearer to one week in London and Paris during April vacation. All tickets, rooms, and red beans & rice will be provided, provided the bearer carries Arvell's bass every once in a while. Ho! Ho! Ho!

Santa Satch

"You're kidding, right?" said Little Fred.

Louis raised his hand. "No way, José. Just don't waltz into any more race riots. And you have to bring your horn, too. Those London and Parisian dollies don't want to hear an old cat like me. They want to lay their eyes on a sharp young dude like yourself."

We'll see about that. He hugged his old friend. "I

can't thank you enough, Louis. I didn't think you'd bring me anywhere after Nashville."

"Thank your father. 'Twas his idea." Louis sipped his cocoa. "So, where's Sarah tonight?"

Big Fred fiddled with the radio dial. A choir singing *Joy to the World* came in clearly. "Her folks live outside of Boston. She's spending the holidays with them."

"She's one fine gal," said Louis. "I've been thinking of adding a singer to my band. Maybe she'd be interested. So . . . how are things going between you two?"

Finally! Someone has asked the question.

"You don't beat around the bush—do you, Pops?"

"What's the point?"

Big Fred sighed. "Things are fine between us. She's a wonderful woman and we've become good friends. Are we in love, though, is what you're asking. Right?"

"Yup."

Here it comes. . . .

"The answer to that question is . . . *No.* We're good friends and that's enough."

"Good enough for who?" asked Louis.

"Good enough for both of us. She's a busy woman with a career that involves traveling and I'm . . . well, the truth is I'm simply not ready to fall in love with anyone. Not yet." Big Fred touched his chest. "Lorraine is still too much in here. Stop, Pops. I know what you're going to say: 'She always will be.' True. But she's so strong in my heart that I just can't think of falling in love with anyone else. It's impossible."

How do I feel about this? I thought I'd be happier. . . .

"How does Sarah feel about this?" asked Louis.

"To be honest, I think she'd welcome a relationship. But she understands how I feel. And she still wants to be my friend."

Louis shot Little Fred a wink. "Despite what our friend here did to her gig?"

"Ha! Yes, despite that. So, you see, we were meant to be good friends—at least for now."

Standing up, Louis stretched his arms and yawned. "Ah, playing Cupid is tiring work. I do believe I'll ramble on home to bed. Miss Lucille's lady cousins must be gone by now."

Standing up, Big Fred shook his old friend's hand. "Thank you, Pops. I needed to be taken out of myself tonight. Thank you."

"That was one fine party, wasn't it? Old Ed Milk cooked it up, that rascal. Called me this morning. For me the choice was easy: Listen to Lucille's lady cousins sip their tea and discuss their latest hair color *or* play my horn for my neighbors. And did you catch sly Brother Milk tonight? Slipping in those wild Thelonious Monk chords to trip up old Satch—on Christmas Eve, no less! That dirty dog. . . ."

At the front door Little Fred hugged his friend. "Happy holidays, Louis. Thank you so much for my present—it doesn't seem real. I'll drop by tomorrow with my present for you and Mrs. Armstrong."

Louis' eyes crinkled as he smiled. "God bless you two—and to all a good night!"

Father and son stood in their doorway, breathing in the frosty air, watching Santa Satch ramble on home.

Twenty-Seven

March 28, 1960. A mild spring evening, the sky awash in purple and rose, the breeze smelling of damp earth. Four boys, now all thirteen years old, throw the ball around on the baseball diamond.

"How long 'til you go?" asked Mark.

"'Bout three weeks," said Fred. "I can't believe it's almost here."

Scooping up a grounder, Mark rifled it over to Steve. "So Trumpetboy gets to spend a week in London and Paris while little Stevie and me spend our vacation stuffing inserts into the *Daily News*. Man, this life ain't fair."

"I'm taller than you," said Steve.

Across the street old Mrs. Fontaine was hunting for one of her cats.

"You said that Louis wants you to play on stage

with him?" said Tim.

"Yeah." *No way. No way. No way.*

"Gonna do it?"

"I don't know." *No way.*

"Hey," said Steve, "at least if you make an idiot of yourself over there you can make a clean getaway."

"Do you practice saying stupid things," asked Tim, "or does the talent just come naturally?"

"Shut up," said Steve.

"Terrific comeback, son. Really witty."

Old Stevie has a point. Nobody knows me in Europe . . . but nobody knew me in the Vanguard either. The very idea of stepping again on a stage made him feel close to vomiting. *Step right up, folks. Pay your money to see Freddie Bradley, the king of the Technicolor yawn. Just don't sit too close to the stage.* He scooped up a grounder and threw to Tim. *Maybe I'll become a dentist. They make good loot.* The streetlights suddenly lit up. *But do I want to have my hands in people's mouths all day?*

"What's Louis doing?"

"Probably packing," said Fred. "He's off tomorrow to Chicago and then all over the place."

"And *then* to London and Paris," said Tim. "Man, being a musician must be the life! Do you realize how lucky you are to have this talent? I took piano lessons for a year and then clarinet lessons for two years and I finally gave up. My dad said my clarinet sounded like fifty buffaloes farting."

"Anyone can do it," said Fred, "if he keeps working at it."

"Wrong," said Tim. "That's like saying that anyone can play football for the Giants. Some talents you're either born with or you're not. *You* are a born musician."

"Thanks." *Tim's a good guy. Why did we used to make so much fun of him? We were so stupid.*

"Let's go over to wish Louis a great trip," said Mark. "I haven't seen the old dude in a while."

When they arrived at 34-56 107th Street, the Armstrongs were sitting in lawn chairs in front of their stoop, sipping lemonade and talking. "It's the Youth Brigade!" chuckled Louis. "Grab some stairs, lads. It's March 28 but it feels like early May. How about some lemonade?"

Dressed in Bermuda shorts, white socks, sandals, and a Duke Ellington t-shirt, Louis slowly stood up. "*Oooooooooooooh.* Not as young a cat as I once was. Back in a mini-flash."

"Are you going to Chicago, too, Mrs. Armstrong?" asked Mark.

Fanning herself with a *TV Guide*, Lucille smiled. "Wouldn't miss it. Somebody has to keep an eye on his old bones. Besides, our second stop is St. Louis, where my sister lives. I'm going to visit with her until Fred and Louis return from Europe."

Leaping up, Fred held the screen door for his friend. Soon they were all drinking lemonade and talking.

"What did you do for fun when you were a kid, Mr. Armstrong?" asked Tim.

"Call me *Louis* or *Pops*, son. To tell you the truth, I mostly worked. Blew my horn and helped my employers, the Karnofskys, gather up rags and bottles and such truck for their business. Any coins I could scrape together I passed on to my mama."

"Must be great living in a big old house now," said Steve.

"Just this morning," said Mrs. Armstrong, "I caught him staring into the ice-box. 'What are you staring at?' I asked. 'Isn't it wonderful?' he said. 'Look at all those eggs. Anytime we want, even in the middle of the night, we can fry us up some fine food.' My husband has dined with royalty yet he's happy that there are eggs in the ice-box."

Louis looked shy. "Once you been poor, man, you don't take nothing for granted. And I mean *nothing*."

"My dad says that New Orleans is one tough town," said Tim. "Did you get into many fights?"

"Not this cat! Little Louis always knew how to stay clear of danger. But, man, *bad dudes* lurked around every corner. My neighborhood was not called *The*

Battlefield for nothing. Let's see.... There was Yellow Lugene, and Dirty Dog, and Long Head Willie Logan, and Jimmy Maker, and Red Devil and so many others. All these cats carried knives to cut you and pistols to shoot you if you looked at 'em funny. Oh, yeah, I can never forget Cheeky Black, who almost killed me for kissing his girl. You never *saw* these chubby legs run so fast! Roughhouse Camel was another one I steered clear from."

"What were you doing kissing Cheeky Black's woman?" demanded Mrs. Armstrong, winking at the boys. "You should've been kissing *me* and you would've stayed out of trouble."

Louis smiled his sweetest smile. "But, my love, you weren't born yet, *heh heh heh.* And don't forget, those New Orleans women were as mean as jungle cats: Cross-Eyed Louise; Mary Jack the Bear; Mary Meat Market; Big Vi Green; Funky Stella; Foote Mama. Oh, my goodness! I'm getting the shakes just remembering!"

The boys were cracking up. "What kind of crazy names are those?" asked Mark.

"Don't let Mary Jack the Bear hear you say that, Pops. She's about ninety-nine these days and she'd cut you sooner than look at you!"

From down the block floated mothers' voices and fathers' whistles calling their children home. It was a school night and it was growing dark.

"I just heard your mama calling you, Steve," said Mark. "Better run off now."

"I didn't hear nothing," said Steve.

"*Steven!*" called a woman's voice. "*Steven! Time for your bath!*"

Mark snickered. "Does your mama climb in the tub with you, too?" However, his snicker didn't last long because soon Mark's mother's voice could also be heard.

"Thanks for the lemonade," said Fred. "Can we help you bring in the cups?"

"Don't bother," said Louis with a wink. "Miss Lucille needs the exercise."

Mrs. Armstrong swatted her husband with her *TV Guide*. "I'll give you exercise, you old dog!"

"That's what I'm hoping, *heh! heh! heh!*"

"Our best to your parents, boys," said Mrs. Armstrong. "Send my love to your father, Fred."

"I will, Mrs. Armstrong."

Gently punching Fred on the arm, Louis said, "It's almost April in Paris time, Pops. Those *mademoiselles* love a man with a horn! So bring *two*—your new one and your Grandpa Henry's."

"I will. Have a great trip, Louis."

As Fred looked back, the old musician and his lady were still in their lawn chairs, laughing at something one of them had said.

Twenty-Eight

April 20, 1960

I can't believe I'm here! This is actually London!

Little Fred leapt from the bed to the thick beige carpet then back up to the bed again. The hotel room's two windows ran all the way to the ceiling, opening like doors onto a balcony overlooking a lush leafy lawn called Green Park. Standing at the railing, Fred looked out upon the ancient city of London. *I'm across the ocean. I'm in another country!*

A door opened and in popped Louis. "Not too shabby, gov'nor," he declared, strutting about. "We've certainly come up in the world. God bless Millie and her fine Nashville establishment, but it sure ain't the Ritz—and this is!"

Fred used the bed as a trampoline. "I just can't believe I'm here."

"Know what you mean. Took me at least five years

of wandering overseas until I grew used to it all. Hey, I'm going to bathe my chops in witch hazel and salve and grab a little nap. I'm right next door, so if you need anything just play a tune on your horn."

Should I ask? "Louis, do you mind if I take a walk around?"

The old musician thought a moment. "Alright. Just be back by five bells. Be dropping breadcrumbs behind you so you can find your way back. I don't want to get a call from the Old Bailey." He winked. "That's a London jail, Pops."

"I swear—no jails. Louis, thanks for this."

"Ah, don't mention it. Glad to have my dear friend along for the ride. Just be back by five. We'll head out into old London town and hunt down some lovely red beans and rice. *Yeah!*"

Fred headed into the shady lanes of Hyde Park. *It's sure quieter than Central Park—but just as beautiful.* At a small café by a stream called the Serpentine, he bought a soda, then relaxed up against a stout leafy oak. *The sky here looks the same as the sky at home. Does the sky over China look the same, too?*

"Excuse me," said an elderly man walking a dog. "Do you have the time?"

Fred checked the watch his father had bought him for the trip. "Two thirty-five, sir."

The old chap nodded. "Thank you, kind sir."

The sky might look the same here—but no New Yorker has ever called me "kind sir"!

Soon he was strolling along a street easily as crowded as Fifth Avenue—Oxford Street. It seemed as if all of London were outdoors on this fine April afternoon: children holding their mothers' hands; businessmen wearing bowler hats and carrying umbrellas; elderly people who had lived through two world wars gazing into store windows. A red stream of double-decker buses and black taxicabs flowed past.

A snug record shop caught his eye. Classical music played inside as customers browsed through the aisles. In the jazz section the Louis Armstrong bin was stocked with many albums, all of which were already in Big Fred's collection. Black and white photographs of the young Louis of the 1920s—the musician who had taught the world to swing—stared out from the album sleeves.

"You fancy jazz, do you?" asked a girl's voice.

Turning, Fred felt the breath from a lovely young face. *What have we here?* She was about his age—with saucy brown eyes; coffee-colored skin; and a frothy spray of black curls—and she was smiling at him.

"Yeah, I love jazz," he replied.

"Oh, so you're a Yank then."

Fred began to laugh.

"And what's so funny?" demanded the young lady.

"Nothing. I'm sorry. I've just never heard a black girl speak with an English accent before, that's all."

"That's because I was born here, Simple Simon. My father is from Morocco and my mum's from Paris." She stuck out her hand. "I'm Ruby."

"I'm Fred. I'm from Corona, Queens. That's part of New York City."

"And what are you doing in a record shop on Oxford Street?"

Man, she's gorgeous. "I'm here with Louis Armstrong. We're here for a few days and then we're heading to Paris."

The girl looked him up and down. "Funny, you don't look like a liar."

To heck with her. Fred began browsing through the Count Basie section. "If you don't believe me, come to the Palladium's stage door tonight. Around eight. Ask for Fred. I'll be there and I might let you in."

"You *are* on the level." She grabbed Basie's *April in Paris* album from his hands. "Can I bring my dad? He's jazz mad."

"Sure. I'll let you both in." *Aren't you the big man! I wish Mark could see this.*

Ruby smiled playfully. "And what are you up to now, Fred from New York?"

"Nothing. Why?" *Remember: Louis said to be back at*

the Ritz by five. You can't let him down.

"Follow me!"

Since Ruby's walk was a trot, Fred had to hustle to keep up. They dashed out the door of the shop and around a corner into an alley. A red motorbike leaned against a brick wall. "Fancy a tour?" she asked.

"Sure. I just have to be back at my hotel by five."

"Plenty of time. Hop on!"

Fred sat behind her. "Once we get rolling," she said, "you're going to have to wrap your arms around me. Don't be a shy guy."

Soon Ruby's red motorbike was whizzing down Oxford Street, weaving in and out of the stalled traffic. Her hair smelled like flowers. *I'm in London. The sun's shining and I have my arms around a beautiful girl's waist. I wonder what Mark and Steve and Tim are doing right now? Probably stuffing inserts into the* Daily News . . . *heh . . . heh . . . heh!*

From the peaceful leafy streets of St. John's Wood to the bustling cafes of Chelsea; from the Houses of Parliament to the narrow streets of Soho; from fluttering, pigeon-filled Trafalgar Square to the bumpy cobblestones of Leicester Square: Fred saw it all from the back of Ruby's motorbike.

For a spell they took a breather on a bench beside the River Thames.

"Funny. . . ," said Ruby.

"What?"

"I just remembered something: When my mum was a girl she once tooled around Paris with a bloke from Duke Ellington's band. He was a sweet kid, too, she said, so she showed him the sights. I'll have to tell her about *you*."

Did she just call me "sweet"? Man!

"So what do Yankee boys do for fun?

"I don't know—just regular stuff. My friends and I play a lot of baseball."

"You play trumpet, too, don't you."

"How did you know that?"

Ruby smiled. "Your upper lip is puckered. My dad plays, too, and his upper lip looks like a triangle. Are you any good?"

"When I play by myself I'm pretty good." He told her about the night in the Village Vanguard. "I just fell apart. I couldn't do it. Louis wants me to play in front of an audience either here or in Paris, but I don't think I can do it."

She brushed away several lovely curls from her eyes. "Why?"

"I don't know—I just freeze up. I see all those eyes looking at me—and meanwhile I have to keep thinking of what I'm playing—and I just fall apart."

"So don't look at them. Turn your back on the audience. Isn't that what Miles Davis does?"

"Yeah, but I'm just a kid. Having Miles turn his back on you is one thing. Having a kid do it would be insulting. Besides, Louis doesn't go for that stuff. He says you should respect your audience."

Ruby rolled her eyes. "So respect your audience, play your horn—and close your eyes. It's quite simple, really." She laughed. "Why do boys make everything so complicated?"

Little Fred had to laugh. "I guess it keeps us busy. So what about you? What does a London girl do for fun?"

Her brown eyes were watching a barge glide beneath the Tower Bridge. "Well, we're doing it, aren't we? Just talking to people and sitting by the river and riding my motorbike around town. It belonged to my mum when she was a girl and when I turned twelve she gave it to me. My dad drives a cab but on Saturday nights he plays his trumpet in a trad-jazz band down at the Pint of Pigs—that's our neighborhood pub—and I love to go down with my mum and dance. His band is pretty good."

Soon they were zipping through the bank-filled streets of Westminster.

"It's four-fifty!" she yelled back. "Where's your hotel?"

"I forget the street's name," yelled Fred, "but it's the Ritz."

"*Wheee!* I'm squiring a rich dude around town!"

"Naw, not me. Louis is paying for everything."

At five o'clock sharp they pulled up in front of the imposing hotel. Reluctantly unwinding his arms, Fred stepped off the motorbike. "Thanks for the tour, Ruby," he said. Looking at the lovely girl smiling at him, he found himself wishing that he, too, were a motorbike-driving citizen of London town. "Do you still want to come to tonight's show?"

"Are you joking? My dad will be over the moon. What time?"

"Well, the show begins at nine. Come to the stage door around eight. I'll try to be there. If not, just ask for me."

Leaning over, Ruby kissed him on the cheek. "Brilliant! See you then, Fred from New York!"

And with a roaring *put-put*, Ruby was gone.

Twenty-Nine

"Our boy's in love, Barney. Just dig that love-sick look!"

Louis, Barney, and Fred were seated at an outdoor Italian restaurant in Covent Garden. The sun was setting as the three friends dined on ravioli and lasagna. ("It's not red beans and rice, but it's not *too* shabby either," Louis declared).

"I'm not in love," said Fred. "I just went for a motorbike ride."

"True—but I do believe a kiss was involved," said Barney.

"On the cheek," said Fred. *Unfortunately!*

Louis sipped his ice tea. "Ah! Splendid vintage! Brother Barney, back me up on this: Is it or is it *not* a fact that those *fine* sweet ladies all dig musicians?"

"Why do you think I picked up a clarinet? To watch those New Orleans dollies come running, that's why.

Even to a moon-faced bald man they come a-running!"

"You say her daddy's coming to tonight's show?" asked Louis.

"I invited both of them. Is that alright?"

"Oh, that's fine as wine, Pops. In fact, I'm glad you did. Now I'll have the opportunity to ask her daddy if the girl's intentions are honorable. *Heh! Heh! Heh!*"

Slapping their knees, the two old musicians laughed until their eyes were teary. "Oh, good Lord!" gasped Louis, wiping his eyes with a handkerchief. "They're both welcome to the show. You know me, Fred. The more folks digging the music the better."

The three dug in, polishing off their meal in no time. Loosening his belt, Fred sat back and watched the people strolling through Covent Garden. Many seemed to recognize Louis, but, being cool Brits, they merely nudged, looked, and strolled on. Nearby church bells were tolling the hour: six o'clock. "Three hours to show time, Barn," said Louis. *Look at all these people*, thought Fred. *Look at them. While I'm living my little life in Corona, they're all here, living their lives. And this is only one section of one city. Think of all the people all over the world. . . .*

Barney chuckled. "Hey, Pops, remember Po-Face Tucker?"

"*Heh, heh*, indeed I do. That man could fall asleep

anywhere, anytime, and it was *impossible* to wake him. A pounding trumpet in his ear couldn't wake old Po-Face."

"One night in New Orleans," said Barney, "he was sleeping so soundly that several of us—your grandfather included, Fred—bought him a train ticket to. . . . Where was it, Pops?"

"Dallas, *heh, heh, heh*."

"That's right. We put poor Po-Face in his seat, tucked a blanket around him, then watched that old train pull out of the station. He told us later that he was well into Texas before he woke up!"

Roaring, the two musicians slapped palms across the table. A passing Englishman in a bowler hat shot them a glance, but Louis and Barney did not notice.

At seven o'clock Fred, nervously cradling his grandfather's trumpet, was sitting in Louis' Palladium dressing room. Wearing green boxer shorts with a purple handkerchief tied around his head, Louis sat before a mirror rubbing salve into his lips. "There's no better way to impress a young lady, Pops, than to play music for her. I know *that* from experience. Now you know *Struttin' With Some Barbecue* cold. You *know* you do."

Fear crept up Fred's throat. *Oh, no, not again.* He placed the trumpet to his lips and blew several notes.

"Come on, Pops," said Louis. "I'll toss you a nifty

little introduction, then you'll trot on out and blow your horn for a few minutes. Nothing could be easier." Fred stared at the black-and-white tiled floor. "I don't mean to be mean, Fred, but if you *do* want to be a musician, you have to conquer this fear of the people. *They're* who you're playing for—not for your four bedroom walls."

"I know."

Standing, Louis put his hand on the boy's shoulder. "I'm not going to nag you anymore, son. You come on out when you feel good and ready. And when you do, you'll realize what I've known since I was your age: that playing music for an audience is the greatest feeling in life. The queasies abandon ship right away and you feel this incredible rush of energy and happiness. *Whew!* I couldn't live without it."

Maybe I'll be a musician who plays alone for his own enjoyment. "Thanks, Louis, but I don't think I'll play tonight. But thanks for understanding."

Maybe I simply don't have what it takes.

"Y'know, it's cruel to encourage a cat who doesn't have the talent. It only prolongs the inevitable—that moment when he has to face the truth." Louis leaned in close. *His eyes are so blood-shot*, thought Fred. *Some nights he looks so beat.* "But that's not the case with you, Fred. You have a genuine gift for music—that's the God's honest truth—and it would be a shame

203

if you never shared that gift with people. It would be like the young woman who has the gift to be the world's greatest surgeon—but her daddy doesn't believe in girls going to college. A dirty shame. But look at old Satch, breaking his own promise not to nag. It's all up to you. The opportunity is there if you want to grab it. If you don't, I'm saving the energy in these old lips for the show."

At eight o'clock the Palladium's front doors were opened. Barney sauntered over. "Where are you meeting your dolly?"

"I told her by the stage door."

"Go on over, lad. Beautiful ladies are not to be taken for granted."

But Ruby and her father were not in the alley outside the stage door. "If you see a girl about my age with her father," Fred asked a security guard. "Could you let her in?"

The man touched the bill of his cap. "Glad to oblige, sir. And what's the young lady's name?"

"Ruby. I don't know her father's name." *Or her last name.*

"Will do, sir."

The crowd stood roaring for over five minutes after Louis appeared onstage. Standing by the musty red stage curtains, Fred tried to look out into the audience but was blinded by the lights on the lip of the stage. "Thank you, folks," Louis said over and over, his smile as bright as the lights. "Thank you, folks."

"*Where is she?*" mouthed Barney from center stage.

"*I don't know,*" Fred mouthed back.

My first date—and I'm being stood up. Figures.

Finally the applause died down. "Thank you kindly, folks. I'm Louis Armstrong. The All Stars and I are here to play some of that good old music for you tonight. So let's go!" Raising his trumpet to his battered lips, Louis blew *The Potato Head Blues* like he was again the young revolutionary of 1927. *He's played these songs hundreds of times—yet he plays each one like it's the first time. Where does he find the energy—and the inspiration?*

The song ended to a thunderstorm of applause. *They whistle more here than they do back home*, thought Fred. "Thank you very much, folks," growled Louis. "This is one for all of you Londoners out there. I assume there's a few of you in the crowd tonight, *heh, heh...*" Holding his trumpet, Louis sang a tender version of the Gershwins' *A Foggy Day* that had the audience sighing before Barney stepped up and swung the song home.

"Thank you kindly," said Louis. "Now here's a good old good one, *Musrat Ramble*, played with style by our very own Trummy."

Beneath the Palladium's ornate ceiling and several chandeliers, Louis and his All Stars played like men possessed. Song followed song and soon it was intermission. Drenched in sweat, Louis drank glass after glass of water, then changed his shirt. His eyes twinkled. "Let's give it to 'em, boys," he growled and Barney, Trummy, Billy, Arvell, and Barrett, like soldiers following their captain into battle, were right behind him.

I guess Ruby's not coming, thought Fred, standing in the wings. *Something must've happened. Maybe she has a boyfriend. Pretty girls usually do.* Louis' golden trumpet showered beams of reflected light as he finished a blistering solo. Twice he glanced over at the boy with a questioning glance. Twice Fred shook his head *No.* Twice Louis shot his friend a wink. *I wonder if I would've gone on stage tonight to impress her. . . . Maybe . . . I don't know . . . Louis is right: I have to do it sometime . . . just not tonight.*

The Londoners brought the American musicians back for five encores. "Sorry, folks," Louis finally shouted into the microphone. "I have no more air left. *Goodnight!*"

The All Stars looked drained yet happy as they strolled offstage. "Where's your dolly?" asked Barney, his bald dome gleaming.

"She never showed up."

Arvell chuckled. "I thought that only happened to Billy."

"I need a shower," growled Louis. "Hey, Fred, can you please find me some orange juice?"

Thirty minutes later Louis was showered, wrapped in a bathrobe, sitting in a chair sipping his juice. "Man, that was one hot show! Who says the English are reserved? Not me! Hey, sorry about your no-show lady friend."

This is embarrassing. "Doesn't matter. I mean, we're leaving for Paris tomorrow anyway."

Seized with an idea, Louis leapt up. "Come on. Let's go for a walk. I'm too jazzed to head back to the hotel. I'll be dressed in a sec."

A huge ivory moon lit up the sky as the two friends strolled the streets of London. Soon they were walking beside the River Thames, the darkened Houses of Parliament and Big Ben's glowing face growing closer with each step.

"It's always a kick to see something up close that you've only seen in photos or movies," said Louis. "That's why I'm patient with people when they see little old me, *heh, heh.*" A couple holding hands strolled by. "My first time in London—let's see . . . twenty eight years ago this month!—I sat on the same bench we'll soon be planting our behinds on. I sat there one drizzly night and just *stared* at Big Ben. I couldn't believe that I was actually here looking up at the old fellow."

A bearded hobo lay asleep beneath a riverside tree. Louis placed a finger against his lips. "*Shhh. . . .*" Digging into his pockets, he crept up to the snoring figure. Slowly bending down, Louis placed a pile of pound notes and various coins in the shadows beside the man.

"Good," he said as they continued on. "Now he'll wake up and believe there's magic in this world."

A few moments later, as a dark barge slid downriver, Louis found his bench. A silhouette standing on deck waved and Fred and Louis waved back. For a long time the two friends were quiet, each lost in his own thoughts.

Louis laughed. "You know, sometimes my life amazes me. *Me!*—Little Louis from The Battlefield!—hanging out in old London town, playing my horn for the people. Who would've guessed that *this* would be my life way back in the Waif's Home? Not me—that's for sure. Now here's the triple truth: If a cat finds his true talent and works hard at it, he can go *any*where in this world. I'm living proof." Another barge slipped past. The ancient city seemed hushed and dreaming. "You know," said Louis, "I always try to plug the *fiiine* times into my memory so that I'll never forget them. Have you ever done that?"

"I don't think so."

"It's easy—like this: *It's April 1960 and my dear friend Fred and I are sitting besides the Thames looking over at Big Ben. I will always remember this moment.*" The clock's face suddenly went black. "Hmm, must be midnight. Okay, so close your eyes and tell yourself that *you* will always remember this moment, too."

A breeze smelling of river water ruffled the boy's shirt. As he closed his eyes, Fred knew that he would never forget a second of this night in London with Louis.

Thirty

By ten o'clock the next morning, the musicians were showered, fed, packed, and ready for Paris. A white limousine was waiting for them in front of the hotel.

Arvell whistled. "Will you *look* at that car! Man, you just *got* to love the Brits."

The sky was a quickly scuttling gray, with an occasional raindrop plopping down on the limo's windshield. Before he climbed in, Fred took one last look around.

"Looking for anyone in particular?" asked Barney.

"Now leave the boy alone," said Louis, "or I'll tell him about some of your—*ahem*—romantic misadventures."

Barney's face fell in mock horror. "You wouldn't!"

"Oh, wouldn't I, *heh, heh*. . . ."

With all the All Stars aboard, the limousine pulled into morning traffic. The driver found a radio station that was playing Duke Ellington's *Mood Indigo*.

"There you are, Barney!" said Billy. "What year would this be?"

"We recorded this so many times, but this sounds like the original from 1930. Man, I had a lot more money back then."

"Not to mention hair," said Arvell.

The driver kept peering into his rear view mirror. "Get a load of this bird," he said. "Does she want to get herself killed?"

Fred turned. Ruby was right behind the limousine, her red motorbike *put-put-puttering* away. "Can we stop for a minute?" he asked.

Checking his watch, Louis grinned. "Five minutes, Loverboy."

"Man," said Arvell, "our Freddie has the ladies chasing *him*!"

The limousine pulled to the curb and Fred stepped out.

"Hi!" said Ruby, breathless and windblown, climbing off the bike. "I've been following you lot for *blocks*. I just wanted to apologize for not showing up last night."

"That's okay," said Fred. "You don't have to apologize."

"But I want to. Y'see, my dad couldn't find his glasses. Then the poor thing banged his head on an open cabinet and bled like a stuck pig. My mum and I had to bring him to hospital for stitching up."

"Is he okay?"

"Yeah. Now he'll be able to brag about his scar down the pub." Ruby reached into her pocket. London traffic whizzed by. "Here's my address. Please let's keep in touch."

"Hey, I write a mean letter."

Leaning over, Ruby kissed him on the cheek. "You're a lovely boy, Fred from New York. Well, I'm off. Cheers!" Hopping back aboard her motorbike, she vanished down the street and around a corner.

"That was one fast woman!" said Arvell.

"I know. I like 'em that way."

"*Aaaaaaaaaaaah!*"

"Now take a gander down there," said Louis. "Those are the White Cliffs of Dover."

Fred looked out the airplane's window at the cold green waters of the English Channel. The bone white cliffs of Dover were growing smaller by the second. "That's where Aunt Betsy lives in *David Copperfield.* She owns a cottage right by the cliffs and is always chasing donkeys off her grass."

"I read it years ago," said Louis. "I loved the movie so much that I just had to read the book." He leaned back and closed his eyes. "Man, I can't wait to see old

Paris. I could've cried during the war—picturing my beautiful city in the hands of the Nazis."

"My dad says that you can't really explain Paris to someone who's never been there," said Fred.

"As usual, your pop is right. Old Paris has to be *experienced* to be believed."

Soon the plane was touching down at Orly Airport. After the musicians breezed through customs, a phalanx of photographers greeted them by the baggage carousel. "*Vive, Lew-eeeee!*" cried a group of fans as the flashbulbs burst around them.

Louis turned on his smile. "*Magnifique! Fantastique! Bardot Brigitte!*"

Piling into two cabs, they were soon on a highway. In the distance Fred could see a white rounded dome. "What's that?" he asked.

"The church of Sacre Coeur," said Billy. "It stands on top of a hill, Montmartre, that overlooks all of Paris."

"We'll be heading up there," said Louis. "Don't you worry."

Their hotel on the rue de l'Harpe was small, clean, and quiet. "We could've stayed at one of the big babies," explained Louis, "but I just love this one so much. Been coming here since 1934."

The owner, a small man with a silver moustache, greeted the old musician with two kisses on each cheek. "Ah, Lew-ee, you're looking well, my friend."

"Now don't you be lying, you old rascal!" said Louis. "Michel, this is Fred. Fred, this is Michel, the owner of the finest hotel in all of Paris."

The old man blushed. "To make sure everything is perfect, I made up the rooms myself. If there is anything you need, just ask."

"There is one thing, Pops: Call up one of your clerks to man the desk tonight because you're coming to my show."

Old Michel bowed. "*Merci, mon ami.*"

Their rooms were on the hotel's top floor. Fred's was small but comfortable with a slanting roof. A fresh April breeze was flowing through a rectangular window built into the ceiling, held open with a metal rod. A sea of chimney-filled rooftops greeted the eye. Across the River Seine the bells of a cathedral were tolling the hour.

"Not the palatial splendor of London town," said Louis, "but this is the real Paris, Pops—not the touristy hotels that might as well be in Akron, Ohio. Not that I'm knocking Akron, you understand. Some mighty fine folks there, too."

"What church is that?" asked Fred.

"Notre Dame Cathedral. Years ago a French cat pulled some strings and I was allowed to blow my horn in there. Man, talk about fine acoustics! The

Frenchmen began building that old fellow in 1163 and didn't finish until over two hundred years later. There must have been great-great-grandsons finishing the work their great-great-grandpappies started." Louis tapped his temple. "Those encyclopedias in my den back home aren't there just 'cause they look nice. Hey, give me a few minutes to wash up. Then I want to show you around."

An hour later the two friends were seated at an outdoor café by the river. It was a breezy afternoon, the sky filled with plump white clouds, as strollers stopped to shake Louis' hand or to merely smile and nod in passing.

"Sometimes I think I'm the luckiest cat in the world," he said after being kissed by two beauties in flowery dresses. "I play my horn all over the world, people know me and respect me, and they even pay me a living wage. It's a gift from God to be a musician, Fred."

"Yeah—and pretty girls kiss you, too."

"*Heh, heh*, now we don't have to tell Miss Lucille about *that!*"

Sitting back, Fred sipped his *citron presse* and watched the stream of Parisians flowing past. *Nearly everyone recognizes Louis!* The old musician greeted one and all with a *Bonjour!* and a smile.

"Look behind you, Pops."

Fred turned. Poking its head above the rooftops, (*like a metal giant*, he thought), stood the Eiffel Tower. "Can we climb to the top?" he asked.

"*You* can. I have a show to blow tonight. I'm taking the elevator."

Little Fred rode the elevator as well and soon the two friends were gazing down at Paris. "Now look to your right. See Notre Dame over there? That's roughly the hoof we have back to the rue de l'Harpe. These old bones might grab a cab. Can you see Sacre Coeur way out there? That's Montmartre, where we'll be heading after tonight's show."

Fred's eyes couldn't drink in the city enough. *Remember this moment. Forever.* "When did you first come here?"

"In 1932. But I came back in the spring of '34 and stayed for three or four months, just lazying around. I didn't feel like recording or even playing many gigs, so I just jammed with some cats from home and even some fine French jazzers. Man, it was *heaven*—like I'd escaped from all of the prejudice and hatred that we black folks can feel back home. I remember this funky café—the *Café Boudon*, it was called—and I'd sit there for hours, just checking out the action. I guess word got around that it was old Satch's crib because musicians would flock around and start conversations and ask advice. For the first time in my *life* folks treated me like an *artist*. I even took to wearing a beret, *heh heh*."

"You *are* an artist, Louis." *A very great one.*

"Thank you, Pops." Louis smiled shyly. "Thanks."

The two friends were quiet for a spell. Fred watched a flock of birds circling over the Seine. *Remember how Mom always talked about going to Paris? 'When we strike it rich your father is bringing me to Paris. You can come, too, Fred.' But she never got here. God, please bless my mother. Please let her know how much I love her.*"

"Louis?"

I don't even want to be a famous musician. I just want to be a musician who gets to come to Paris at least once a year.

"Hmm?"

"I think I'm going to play *Struttin'* with you and the band tonight."

Maybe twice.

Louis' laughter might have been heard by the pilot of the biplane that was lazily aloft in the blue spring-time skies over Paris.

Thirty-One

"*Struttin' With Some Barbecue* isn't that hard to play, Pops."

Maybe not for you. Should I say it? Yes: "Maybe not for you."

"Just don't let your brain get in the way."

Planting his feet, Fred blew his trumpet smooth and mellow, the way Louis had taught him. ("You're a smooth and mellow dude," he'd said during an early lesson, "so that's the way your music will sound").

Old Michel had delivered their dinners to the room and Louis wolfed his down. "Not hungry, Pops?" he asked.

"No," said Fred. "I'll eat after the show." *If I'm not running away.*

"Relax. You're sounding fine." Louis checked his watch. "It's nearly seven. We have to split for the Salle Pleyel soon, but let's run through the song one more time."

A black limousine was waiting for them outside the hotel. "Where are the guys?" asked Fred as he climbed in the backseat. He had brought both his new trumpet and his grandfather's.

"Already at the theater—although with Barney, I'm never sure. He could be out in Montparnasse scarfing down some good old red beans and rice. Barn's a New Orleans cat like me."

Fred looked out the window at the passing Boulevard St. Michel. "It's warm for April," said Louis, "but even if it were chilly everyone would be out like this. I don't think Parisians stay home much." He chuckled. "But there's so much going on, why would they want to?" On every block was an outdoor café bursting with customers. Everywhere people were sitting, chatting, sipping wine, sipping coffee. *But it's calmer, slower here than in New York,* thought Fred. The last rays of sunlight were fading and the lights were switching on in the cafes and restaurants. Rolling down his window, Fred breathed in: The air smelled of bus exhaust and freshly brewed coffee.

"Got them heebie-jeebies?" asked Louis.

"I'm terrified, Louis."

"Can I tell you about my worse case of 'em?"

"Sure." *Was Louis ever nervous—of anything?*

"It was about eleven o'clock on a steamy August night in 1922—Lord, I'll never forget it!—when my train pulled into Chicago. I was just a kid, been muching for days on trout loaf sandwiches made by my mama, God rest her, and anyone looking at me knew in a *flash* that I was a country boy."

"Why were you in Chicago?" asked Fred as they passed over the Seine.

"Because Joe Oliver, my musical daddy, had sent for me. Probably the only soul who I would've left old New Orleans for.

"So I'm standing all alone in Union Station, holding my horn in one hand and my little suitcase in the other. I know that King Oliver's Creole Jazz Band is playing at a place called the Lincoln Gardens, but I don't know which way to turn. Luckily, though, Papa Joe had tipped off several porters to keep an eye peeled for a chubby rube holding a horn. One gentleman finds me, plops my behind in a cab, and tells the driver where to go.

"The Lincoln Gardens was on the South Side of town, so I'm standing on the pavement *outside* hearing all that good swinging music from *inside*, too terrified to venture in. We didn't have fancy clubs like this back home and I'm just staring there open-mouthed at all the colorful lights and the fancy-dressed ladies in the lobby."

"What did you do?" asked Fred.

"Look over to your left, Pops. That's the Louvre.

We're heading there tomorrow. What did I do? Well, I probably would've turned tail and fled back home. But somebody must have told Papa Joe about the bumpkin standing out in front because here he comes shouting, 'You little fool! We been waitin' for your so-and-so be-hind *all night*. Come on in here!'

"The Lincoln Gardens is all lit up like one of those tales from the *Arabian Nights*. My eyes are just drinking it all in. And up on the bandstand waving me on are some of my homeboys from New Orleans like Johnny Dodds and his brother Baby. Well, you *know* they made Little Louis feel right and ready, so I put that horn to my lips and blew like a hurricane all night!"

"You weren't scared?"

"Man, I was petrified like wood! But I poured those nasty nerves into my performance. And once I'd played ten sweet notes there was no reason why I couldn't play ten thousand more! So the show was *sol-id* and about three in the morning I went home with Papa Joe. What really knocked me out was that his beautiful wife, Mama Stella, had cooked up some of that good old red beans and rice with cornbread and ice cold lemonade. *Hmmmm!* Now t*hat* sure made a boy feel at home!" His eyes closed, Louis smiled at the memory. "After both of us had scarfed for quite a spell, Papa Joe took me by taxi to a boardinghouse that he'd found for me at, let me see, 3412 South Wabash. How's that for a memory? When Papa Joe told me that I had my *own room* with a private bath, guess what I said?"

"*Thanks?*" guessed Fred.

"Nope! I asked, 'What's a *private bath?*' *Heh, heh, heh!* Naturally I knew about rusty old washtubs in the alleys down home, but I'd never heard of a bathtub in my entire twenty-two years. Imagine that!"

Their limousine had pulled in front of a theater that to Fred looked as bright and imposing as the Lincoln Gardens must have looked to Louis Armstrong in 1922.

"So you see, Pops, I was terrified, too. But I took a deep breath, closed my eyes, dove in, and everything has turned out pretty rosy since. Come on, grab your horns. I'm *itching* to play some good music!"

Thirty-Two

I can do this.

Dressed in green boxer shorts, his head covered by a red handkerchief, Louis opened the dressing room's closet door. Inside hung a small black tuxedo. "Your dad gave me the measurements one night when we were watching the Yankees game in your living room. Just call me *Old Sneaky Satch. Heh, heh!*"

"I've never worn a tux before." *I can do this.* His fingers trembled over the buttons. *I can do this.*

Louis grinned. "*That* is some super-slick monkey suit, Pops. How does it feel?"

"Like it has its hands around my throat."

"Welcome to the world of the concert *artiste*. By the way, have you decided which trumpet you're going to use?"

"If you don't mind, I think I'll use my grandfather's. It's harder to play, but I just feel like using it."

Fred found himself wrapped in a bear hug. "Good move, Pops. Old Henry would be proud. I can't blame your dad for feeling bitter, but your grandfather had a *truckload* of fine qualities, too."

A quick knock on the door and Billy, the All Stars' pianist, stuck his head in. "Um, Pops? Do you mind if I have tonight off? I met this sweet *mademoiselle* this afternoon and, *man,* I'd love to hit the town with her."

With only one leg in his pants, Louis was hopping mad. "And what am I supposed to do for a piano player?"

Opening the door wide, Billy laughed. "Will this dude do?"

In the doorway, immaculate in a sky-blue suit, his smile a mile wide, stood Duke Ellington.

"Good Lord!" cried Louis, rushing to put both legs into his pants so he could embrace his old friend. "I thought you were in Venice tonight, Pops!"

"Tomorrow night, lad," said Duke smoothly. "And since I was free this evening, I caught a plane with one goal in mind: to allow William here to squire his fair lady through an evening she will never forget."

With a whoop, Billy was gone. *So this is Duke Ellington. Man, he's tall!* The composer shook Fred's hand. "My boy, it's a pleasure. Pops says that you're a gifted musician."

"Thank you, Mr. Ellington."

"No *misters*, please. We're all musicians here. *Your Excellency* will do."

Fred found himself laughing as easily as the two men. With a laugh, Barney burst in. "Hello, Guv'nor," he said, embracing his old boss.

"Mister *Bigaaaaaaaaaaaaaaard*, I presume? You're looking as bald as ever."

"And the bags beneath your eyes are bigger than ever," said Barney.

Duke smiled his sardonic smile. "I lose sleep at night thinking of all that copious money that flew from my wallet to yours."

Everything he says sounds sarcastic. But it doesn't sound mean.

Louis buttoned up his white shirt. "Old Fred's a tad nervous tonight. He's joining us for *Struttin' With Some Barbecue*. His baptism, so to speak."

Duke flopped down in an easy chair. "Believe me, Fred, you'll be so excited when you hear that applause that you'll want to play a *second* tune. Do you know *Concerto for Cootie*?"

Fred smiled. "Yes, sir, I know it." He had memorized every note, every nuance of Cootie Williams' solo on this 1940 masterpiece.

"Well, if you're up for it," said Duke, "when *Barbecue* is over just let me know with a nod and we'll dive into

Concerto. That is, if it's okay with Mr. Armstrong. It's his gig, after all."

Seated before a mirror, Louis was rubbing salve into his lips. "You cats can play all night if you want. I could use a vacation."

I can do this. I can do this.

After slipping into a pair of shiny black shoes, Fred stood before Louis. "Do I look okay?"

"Even finer than Duke!" chuckled Louis. "Here, you need the final touch." Pinning a red carnation onto Fred's jacket, the old musician looked into the boy's eyes. "I'm proud of you, Pops. Remember that."

I can do this.

Fred embraced his friend. "Thanks, Louis. For everything."

For once, Louis had nothing to say—but his eyes said it all.

Fred saw his reflection in the dressing room mirror. It looked scared. "I'm just going to find a quiet corner and warm up."

Duke winked. "I'd be willing to bet all of Barney's money that you'll be playing *Concerto for Cootie* tonight."

Picking up his two trumpets, Fred headed for the door. "I hope so."

I know I can do this. I'm going to close my eyes, take a deep breath, and play my grandfather's trumpet. Real notes are going to fly out of it and I'm not going to run. I can do this.

Backstage was muggy and musty, the sounds of the entering audience bouncing off the concrete walls. Finding a bench in a dark corner, Fred sat down. Raising his grandfather's horn to his lips, he softly blew *Shenendoah*, his mother's favorite song. "I'm so proud of you," she had said not long before the end. "You've been so strong and brave for me. Just don't be afraid to let it out and cry. Cry like you'll burst. But also know that you don't need to be afraid of *anything*, Fred. There's not much that life can throw at you that will be more difficult than this."

I can do this! This is nothing compared to . . . other things.

As more and more people—chatting, coughing, laughing—filled the Salle Pleyel, Fred seemed to grow calmer. Closing his eyes, he said a prayer for his mother and father.

From far away, a man's voice was speaking French. Then a sudden eruption of applause greeted Louis and the band. *This is it!* Stepping gingerly in the darkness to the side of the stage, Fred watched from beside the rolled-back red curtains. Duke quickly took his seat at the piano, his back to the audience. From behind his bass, Arvell shot Fred a wink.

"*Bon soir, chats et mademoiselles,*" said Louis. "Get

ready 'cause we're going to swing tonight! One, two, three, *four!*"

The band tore into *Tiger Rag*. Barney closed his eyes, raised his clarinet to the heavens, and blew. Watching his compatriots, Trummy placed subtle fills into the music, waiting for his moment to wail. Arvell and Barrett kept the rhythm rock solid while Duke played piano like a Harlem stride master. And Louis, his feet planted like a boxer's, transformed his trumpet—simple metal and valves—into liquid lightning. His sound filled the ears and hearts of every soul in the theater. He played with all of his huge heart and soul, and his men weren't too far behind.

"Thank you kindly, folks!" cried Louis at song's finish. The French were wilder than the British—whistling, stomping, even screaming. "Now here's something to soothe yourselves," he said before launching into a mellow *April in Paris*.

Standing in the wings, Fred watched his friend hold several thousand strangers captive. *I'm not as frightened as I was in the Vanguard. Why?* As song followed song, it was clear that this was a special night. Mopping his face with the fourth of many handkerchiefs, Louis looked over at Fred. As the boy flashed the *okay* sign, the old musician smiled a smile of pure joy. *This is what I want to do with the rest of my life. I might as well begin now.* Stepping up to the microphone, Louis said, "Folks, we have a special guest here tonight to join us on a good old good one called *Struttin' With Some Barbecue*. No doubt you'll be hearing a great deal from him in the years to come. Please give a huge hand to *Fred Bradley!*"

I can do this!

Fred could barely feel his feet moving. *Man, it's hot out here.* The white lights on the lip of the stage were blinding. The audience seemed only a breathing, rustling presence beyond. *I can do this.* When he reached center stage, Louis wrapped an arm around him. "You begin with straight melody, son, and I'll play some harmony beneath you," he said in Fred's ear before turning to the band. "Let's swing it, boys!" he growled. "One, two, three, *four!*"

And they were off.

Taking a deep breath—*Here we go!*—Fred raised Old Henry's trumpet to his lips and blew a clean, well-executed chorus. *Actual music is coming from my horn! That wasn't perfect—but it wasn't half bad.* He held the last note for an extra beat and the people beyond the blinding white lights applauded. *I did it!* Each musician then said his piece—Barney on clarinet; followed by Trummy on trombone; followed by Duke; followed by Louis on blazing, soul-stirring trumpet. His face gleaming with sweat, Louis blew one last glistening note, then nodded to Fred and stepped back.

You can do this!

Closing his eyes, the boy followed Louis' advice: *Think of someone or something you truly love when you play music and you can't go wrong.* He thought of his mother and father, of how much they loved him, and of Louis, and he knew that the music pouring out of his grandfather's horn was honest and strong—his *own* spirit, his *own* life. When he had told his story, Fred stepped back, nodded to Louis, and the entire band took the song home in style.

You did it!

To Fred, standing beside Louis, the applause seemed to last forever.

"My Gaaaawd!" the old musician growled into the microphone. "I better get to practicing!" Wrapping an arm around the boy, Louis leaned down. "I am so proud of you, son."

Peering out into the white lights, Fred was proud of himself. *I don't have to be afraid anymore. I played music in front of an audience in Paris and I can do it again!*

The applause had finally died down when a fresh burst shook the theater. For a moment Fred thought this new round was also for him. But then he smelled Duke's cologne and felt the composer's hand on his shoulder. Louis shouted into the microphone: "I guess we can't keep our little secret any longer, folks. Here he is: *Duke Ellington!*"

"Ladies and gentlemen," said Duke into the maelstrom, "I had a modest wager with Fred here. I told him that if he survived his first song then he could have a go at *Concerto for Cootie*. What do you say? Did he survive *Struttin'*?"

The whistling and stomping of feet told everyone that Fred had indeed survived with style.

Placing a mute inside the bell of his horn, Louis leaned over and said, "You play open, Pops, and I'll play Lady Mute."

Duke counted off and instantly Fred was up to his neck in Ellington's famous *Concerto*. A winding, eloquent piece of music, it took every ounce of the boy's concentration to play. *This is so much fun!* He dove in, pouring his heart into the music. With each golden note his confidence grew. At one point his and Louis' harmonies were as tightly wound as the colors on a barber's pole. *Concentrate!* he told himself, *Don't get cocky!* and as the last note faded, Little Fred was positive that he had just played the finest music of his life.

"Let's hear it for my dear friend Fred Bradley!" roared Louis above the crowd. As a happily dazed Fred wandered offstage, every member of the band, with the exception of Duke, shook his hand. Ellington embraced him.

I can do this!

I'm a musician!
Remember this moment!

Thirty-Three

Corona, Queens: Early July 1960. A humid, orangy-sky evening alive with crickets. Down the street old Mrs. Fontaine was calling for her cats. Little Fred, Big Fred, and Sarah sat on the Bradleys' front stoop, watching the fireflies and eating Good Humor ice cream.

"Was Louis exaggerating?" asked Big Fred. "Did the man really eat *that* much?"

Sarah, her mouth full of ice cream, nodded her head again and again. "*Mgmnmmmmmmmmmggggm-mmmmmnnnnnn.*"

"We'll return to you later," said Big Fred.

"I couldn't believe my eyes, Dad," said his son. "We took a taxi after the show up to Montmartre—me, Louis, Duke, and Barney. The restaurant looked out over the entire city. And when Duke began ordering, our waiter signaled for another guy to come over to help him—he ran out of room on his pad! Duke's eyes were closed and he just went on and on and on: 'I'll begin with a bowl of chicken soup and some hash and scrambled eggs. Then let's follow that up with two of your finest steaks. But could I also have three helpings of mashed potatoes with that, please?'"

"Unbelievable!" said Big Fred.

"But he wasn't done! *Then* he ordered a fish dinner with a side order of lamb chops. 'And I'll follow that up with a chef's salad and a kettle of boiling water with two lemons'!"

"Whooooeeee!"

"And then he ate a *mountain* of peach ice cream for dessert! I was ready for him to be sick or something, but he kept on talking with Louis about some guy named Bubber."

Sarah's ice cream was swallowed. "My mother was good friends with Ivie Anderson, who sang for years with Duke. When I was a girl I'd go with my mother to Ivie's Chicken Shack, a restaurant she owned after she left the band. One time in the kitchen she began to laugh. 'See all of this fried chicken being cooked up? This is enough to serve almost ten customers. But I've seen Duke Ellington eat this much in a single sitting!' I've never forgotten that."

"Did she teach you to sing?" asked Little Fred.

"Ivie taught me how to sing *jazz,* how to let go and improvise. She'd always say: 'Singing jazz is like being free to wander in a lovely, mysterious garden where you never know what's going to pop out.' But I learned how to sing *period* in my church. The training was invaluable."

"Especially now that you've joined Louis' band," said Big Fred. "You're going to have to belt it out to be heard over Pops' horn."

"Actually no, I won't. When Louis accompanies a singer, he's the most mellow, understated musician around. Well, speak of the devil. . . ."

A familiar figure in Bermuda shorts, white socks, and sandals was approaching from down the sidewalk. *Man, he's walking slowly,* thought Little Fred.

"Can I fix you a plate, Pops?" asked Big Fred as the old musician eased himself down on the bottom step of the stoop. "Sarah cooked up a delicious yardbird."

"No, thanks, Fred. Miss Lucille cooked up yet another super-fine pot of red beans and rice. I just dropped by to say *faretheewell.* We're leaving early in the morning for Philly. Can Lucille and I still pick you up, Sarah?"

"If it's no trouble, Pops."

"No trouble at all." Louis wiped his forehead with a red handkerchief. "Hot, ain't it? And that's a New Orleans boy talking."

"You look tired," said Little Fred.

"I *am*, Pops, I am."

"Why don't you just stay home and rest up for awhile?" asked Big Fred.

"Ah, and just get on Miss Lucille's nerves? Nosiree, I'm off to play some music in the City of Brotherly Love. And you know it's always the same story. I'm dog-tired on the plane or the bus, but when I pull into town and see those empty seats and know that in a few hours they'll be filled with folks who paid hard-earned bread to hear me blow my horn . . . well, you *know* that's just *got* to energize an old cat like me. And it *does*, every time."

For a while the four of them were quiet, listening to the crickets. A woman from a nearby porch laughed. From several radios came the roar of the crowd at Yankee Stadium.

"Big Fred, when's your vacation time this year?" asked Louis.

"The first two weeks of August."

"Thought so. Any plans?"

Big Fred looked at his son. "Nothing really. Fred and I were talking about driving up to Cooperstown, but we haven't planned anything yet."

Reaching into a pocket, Louis pulled out an envelope. "How about flying down to Rio de Janeiro on August 2? I just *happen* to have two plane tickets here. Oh, and there's a mighty fine suite reserved for you two in the Copacabana Palace on the *Avenue Atlantica*."

An astonished father and son looked at each other. "Did you know about this?" Big Fred asked Sarah.

Smiling, she said, "Sorry. I'm hard of hearing. What did you say?"

"Oh, but there's just one catch," said Louis with a sly grin.

"What's that?"

"Little Fred here *has* to bring his horns. Seems that those lovely Brazilian ladies own *all* of his records and they'll tear the theater to *bits* if he's not there to blow a tune or two. Plus I know the boy's father would simply love to hear his son play music before an audience."

"Without throwing up," said Little Fred.

"Or running away," added Sarah.

Big Fred reached for Louis' hand. "Pops, you've been there for me and mine my whole *life*. Sometimes I wonder how I could ever repay you for all you've done."

The old musician seemed shy. "*Repay* me?" he growled. "Are you *kidding* me, man? Along with Miss Lucille, you folks are my *family*. Don't you know that? You repay me every day." The red handkerchief fluttered across his face before nestling in a pocket.

"Lord, it's probably cooler in old Brazil right now." Louis clapped his hands. "So, do we have a deal?"

They had a deal.

The Musicians (and Poets and Rebels) Traveling with Louis

Louis Armstrong (1901-1971) (also known as "Dipper," "Satch," "Satchmo," and, his favorite, "Pops"): Jazz music's greatest virtuoso and quite possibly the most influential musician (and singer) of the twentieth century. "Louis Armstrong," said Duke Ellington, "was born poor, died rich, and never hurt anyone on the way."

Barrett Deems (1915-1998): A white man with no bigotry in his soul, Barrett played his beloved drums on a weekly basis right up to his death at the age of 83. "Playing with Pops," he once said, "was a joy every night."

Dizzy Gillespie (1917-1993): In the early 1940s, Dizzy—along with Charlie Parker, Thelonious Monk, and Kenny Clarke—developed a new style of jazz called Bebop. Although the beboppers at first called the musicians of Armstrong's generation *moldy figs*, Diz and Louis became tight friends.

Langston Hughes (1902-1967): One of America's greatest poets, Hughes' poems such as "A Dream Deferred," "I Too Sing America," and "Theme for English B" can be viewed free online.

Billy Kyle (1914-1966): An underrated pianist, Billy played with the John Kirby Sextet and with Sy Oliver before joining the All Stars in 1953. He was on tour with Louis when he died.

John Lewis (1940-present): Since 1987, John Lewis has represented the 5th District of Georgia in the United States House of Representatives. As a young man, he was an influential leader in the SNCC (Student Non-violent Coordinating Committee) as well as a Free-dom Rider. On March 7, 1965—a day known as *Bloody Sunday*—police fractured Lewis' skull at the Edmund Pettus Bridge in Selma, Alabama. John Lewis' auto-biography, *Walking with the Wind*, is among the most powerful books I have ever read. You should read it, too.

Max: based on the great Max Gordon (1903-1989), for many years the owner of the hallowed Village Vanguard. Max's autobiography, *Live at the Village Vanguard*, is es-sential jazz reading. Today his widow, Lorraine Gor-don, runs the basement night club. The next time you're in New York City, ask your parents to bring you to the Vanguard for a set or two of superb music.

Arvell Shaw (1923-2002): Louis' bassist was a "rock-solid rhythm-section bass player," according to Michael Cogswell. When Arvell was a child, his father brought him to a Louis Armstrong concert. "When Louis walked out on that stage and started playing," Arvell recalled, "it was like an electric shock went up my spine."

Trummy Young (1912-1984): After playing his unique style of jazz trombone with Earl Hines and Jimmy Lunceford, Trummy played with the All Stars until 1964. "It was an honor and a pleasure to play with Pops," he once said.

Songs Mentioned in Travels with Louis

"A Foggy Day" (George and Ira Gershwin); recorded by Louis Armstrong and Ella Fitzgerald, 1956

"All of Me" (S. Simons–G. Marks); recorded by Louis Armstrong & His All Stars, 1955

"April in Paris" (Vernon Duke–E.Y. Harburg); recorded by Louis Armstrong and Ella Fitzgerald, 1956

"Black and Blue" (A. Razaf–F. Waller); recorded by Louis Armstrong, 1929

"Concerto for Cootie" (Duke Ellington); recorded by Duke Ellington & His Famous Orchestra, 1940

"Dipper Mouth Blues" (L. Armstrong–J. Oliver); recorded by King Oliver's Creole Jazz Band, 1923

"Dizzy Atmosphere" (Dizzy Gillespie); recorded by Dizzy Gillespie and Charlie Parker, 1945

"Groovin' High" (Dizzy Gillespie); recorded by Dizzy Gillespie and Charlie Parker, 1945

"Honeysuckle Rose" (A. Razaf–F. Waller); recorded by Louis Armstrong & His All Stars, 1955

"Just A-Sittin' and A-Rockin'" (Duke Ellington–Billy Strayhorn–Lee Gaines); recorded by Duke Ellington & His Famous Orchestra, 1941

"Muskrat Ramble" (E. Ory–R. Gilbert); recorded by Louis Armstrong & His All Stars, 1956

"Potato Head Blues" (L. Armstrong); recorded by Louis Armstrong's Hot 7, 1927

"Royal Garden Blues" (C. Williams–S. Williams); recorded by Louis Armstrong & His All Stars, 1956

"Stardust" (H. Carmichael); recorded by Louis Armstrong, 1930

"St. Louis Blues" (W.C. Handy); recorded by Louis Armstrong & His All Stars, 1954

"Struttin' With Some Barbecue" (L. Hardin); recorded by Louis Armstrong's Hot 5, 1927

"Tin Roof Blues" (W. Melrose–B. Pollack–G. Brunies–L. Roppolo–P. Mares–M. Stitzel); recorded by

Songs

Louis Armstrong & His All Stars, 1955

"Twelfth Street Rag" (J.S. Sumner–E.A. Bowman); recorded by Louis Armstrong & His All Stars, 1956

"Time After Time" (Jule Styne–Sammy Cahn); recorded (perfectly) by Tony Bennett on his 1992 album, *Perfectly Frank*

"West End Blues" (C. Williams–J. Oliver); recorded by Louis Armstrong's Hot 5, 1928

The Author

Portrait by Hannah Carlon

Mick Carlon is well into his third decade as a public school English teacher at both the high and middle school levels. When not grading papers, he can be found driving his wife, Lisa, and daughters, Hannah and Sarah, crazy with his incessant playing of jazz CDs. "Jazz musicians are among America's most fearless artists, and if young people will only give the music of artists such as Louis Armstrong a try, they will make an enriching friend for life." Mick's first children's novel, *Riding on Duke's Train,* is about a boy's adventures traveling with Duke Ellington and His Famous Orchestra.

Links

Visit Leapfrog Press on Facebook
Google: Facebook Leapfrog Press

Leapfrog Press Website
www.leapfrogpress.com

Author Website
www.mickcarlon.com

About the Type

This book was set in Adobe Caslon, a typeface originally released by William Caslon in 1722. His types became popular throughout Europe and the American colonies, and printer Benjamin Franklin used hardly any other typeface. The first printings of the American Declaration of Independence and the Constitution were set in Caslon. .

Designed by John Taylor-Convery
Composed at JTC Imagineering, Santa Maria, CA